I0546518

POETRY FROM CRESCENT MOON

Walking In Cornwall
by Ursula Le Guin

Hymns To the Night
by Novalis

Hymns To the Night: In Translation
by Novalis

Flower Pollen: Selected Thoughts
by Novalis

Novalis: His Life, Thoughts and Works
by Novalis

Edmund Spenser: *Heavenly Love: Selected Poems*
selected and introduced by Teresa Page

Edmund Spenser: *Amoretti*
edited by Teresa Page

The Visions of Petrarch and Bellay: Early Sonnets
by Edmund Spenser

Robert Herrick: *Delight In Disorder: Selected Poems*
edited and introduced by M.K. Pace

Robert Herrick: *Hesperides*
edited and introduced by M.K. Pace

Robert Herrick: *Upon Julia's Breasts: Love Poems*
edited and introduced by M.K. Pace

Sir Thomas Wyatt: *Love For Love: Selected Poems*
selected and introduced by Louise Cooper

John Donne: *Air and Angels: Selected Poems*
selected and introduced by A.H. Ninham

D.H. Lawrence: *Being Alive: Selected Poems*
edited with an introduction by Margaret Elvy

D.H. Lawrence: *Amores*
edited with an introduction by Margaret Elvy

D.H. Lawrence: *Look! We Have Come Through!*
edited with an introduction by Margaret Elvy

D.H. Lawrence: *Love Poems and Others*
edited with an introduction by Margaret Elvy

D.H. Lawrence: *New Poems*
edited with an introduction by Margaret Elvy

D.H. Lawrence: *Symbolic Landscapes*
by Jane Foster

D.H. Lawrence: *Infinite Sensual Violence*
by M.K. Pace

Percy Bysshe Shelley: *Paradise of Golden Lights: Selected Poems*
selected and introduced by Charlotte Greene

Thomas Hardy: *Her Haunting Ground: Selected Poems* edited, with an introduction by A.H. Ninham

Thomas Hardy: *Late Lyrics and Earlier* edited, with an introduction by A.H. Ninham

Thomas Hardy: *Moments of Vision* edited, with an introduction by A.H. Ninham

Thomas Hardy: *Poems of the Past and the Present* edited, with an introduction by A.H. Ninham

Thomas Hardy: *Satires of Circumstance* edited, with an introduction by A.H. Ninham

Thomas Hardy: *Time's Laughingstocks* edited, with an introduction by A.H. Ninham

Thomas Hardy: *Wessex Poems* edited, with an introduction by A.H. Ninham

Sexing Hardy: Thomas Hardy and Feminism by Margaret Elvy

Emily Bronte: *Darkness and Glory: Selected Poems* selected and introduced by Miriam Chalk

John Keats: *Bright Star: Selected Poems* edited with an introduction by Miriam Chalk

John Keats: *Poems of 1820* edited with an introduction by Miriam Chalk

Henry Vaughan: *A Great Ring of Pure and Endless Light: Selected Poems* selected and introduced by A.H. Ninham

The Crescent Moon Book of Love Poetry edited by Louise Cooper

The Crescent Moon Book of Mystical Poetry in English edited by Carol Appleby

The Crescent Moon Book of Nature Poetry From Langland to Lawrence edited by Margaret Elvy

The Crescent Moon Book of Metaphysical Poetry edited and introduced by Charlotte Greene

The Crescent Moon Book of Elizabethan Love Poetry edited and introduced by Carol Appleby

The Crescent Moon Book of Romantic Poetry edited and introduced by L.M. Poole

Brigitte's Blue Heart by Jeremy Reed

Claudia Schiffer's Red Shoes by Jeremy Reed

By-Blows: Uncollected Poems by D.J. Enright

THE DISCIPLES AT SAIS

Novalis

THE DISCIPLES AT SAIS

Novalis

Translated by F.V.M.T. and U.C.B.

Edited by Carol Appleby

CRESCENT MOON

First published 1903. This edition 2021. Reprint 2023.

Design by Radiance Graphics
Set in Bodoni Book 11 on 14pt.

British Library Cataloguing in Publication data available for this title.

ISBN-13 9781861718105
ISBN-13 9781861718914

Crescent Moon Publishing
P.O. Box 1312
Maidstone, Kent
ME14 5XU, Great Britain
www.crmoon.com

CONTENTS

NOTE ON THE TEXT

The text is from *The Disciples At Sais and Other Fragments* by Novalis, translated by F.V.M.T. and U.C.B. and published by Methuen, London in 1903.

Novalis

THE DISCIPLES AT SAIS

Men travel by many different paths. Whoever tracks and compares their ways will see wonderful figures arising; figures that seem to belong to the great Manuscript of Design which we descry everywhere, on wings of birds, on the shells of eggs, in clouds, in snow, in crystals, in rock formations, in frozen water, within and upon mountains, in plants, in beasts, in men, in the light of day, in slabs of pitch and glass when they are jarred or struck, in filings around a magnet, and in the singular Coincidences of Chance. In these things we seem to catch an idea of the key, the grammar to this Manuscript, but this idea will not fix itself into any abiding conception, and seems as if it were unwilling to become in its turn the key to higher things. It seems as though an *Alcahest* had been poured over the mind of man. Only momentarily do his wishes, his thoughts, incorporate themselves. On such wise do his ideas arise, but, after a short while, all swims once more vaguely before his eyes.

From afar I heard one say: "Unintelligibility originates in Unintelligence. This seeks what it already has, and therefore attains to nothing further. Speech is not understood, because speech does not understand itself, and will not be understood. Genuine Sanscrit speaks for the sake of speaking, because speech is its pleasure and its essence."

Not long after this another said: "Holy Writ needs no commentary. Whoso speaks truly is full of everlasting life, and his Evangel seems to us wonderfully linked with Genuine Secrets, for it is a harmony out of the Universal Symphony."

The Voice must certainly have spoken of our Master, for he knows how to collect the indications that are scattered on all sides. A singular light kindles in his glance when the sublime Rune is unrolled before us, and he looks discerningly into our eyes to find out whether for us too the Star has arisen that shall render the Figure visible and comprehensible. If he see us sad, that our night is not breaking, he comforts us and promises future joy to the faithful and assiduous seer. Often he has told us how, as a child, the impulse to exercise the faculties, to occupy and satisfy them, left him no peace. He looked up to the stars and imitated in the sands their positions and their courses. He gazed into the aërial sea without pause and was never weary of contemplating its transparency, its agitations, its clouds, its lights. He collected stones, flowers and every sort of insect, and set them out in many-fashioned lines. He watched men and animals; he sat by the sea-shore gathering shells. He listened heedfully to his own heart and to his thoughts. He knew not whither his longing was driving him. When he was older he wandered, beholding other countries, other seas, new skies, strange stars, unknown plants, animals and men; he descended into caves and marked how in courses and coloured strata the Edifice of the Earth had been built up. He manipulated clay into wonderful rock forms. At this time he found everywhere objects already known to him but marvellously mingled and mated, and strange vicissitudes often arose within him. Soon he became aware of the inter-relation of all things, of conjunctions, of coincidences. Ere long he saw nothing singly. The perceptions of his senses thronged together in great variegated Pictures; he heard, saw, felt and thought simultaneously. He took pleasure in bringing strangers together. Sometimes the stars became men to him, men as stars; stones were as animals, clouds as plants; he sported with forces and phenomena; he knew where and how he could find and bring to light this or that, and thus himself plucked at the strings in his search for tones and sequences. What came to him after this he does not make known to us. He tells us that we ourselves, led on by him and by our own desire, may discover what happened to him. Many of us forsook him. They returned to their parents and learnt to follow a trade. Some have been sent forth by him we know not whither; he chose them out. Of these some had been there but a short time, others longer. One was still a child. Scarcely was he there but the Master wished to resign the teaching into his hands. This child had great dark eyes with blue depths; his skin shone like lilies, and his locks like lustrous cloudlets at eventide. His voice thrilled through our hearts; we would have gladly given him our flowers, stones, feathers, all that we had. He smiled with an infinite gravity; we felt strangely happy to be beside him. One day he will return, said the Master, and live among us. Then the lessons will cease. He sent another pupil with him who often made us impatient. He seemed ever sorrowful. Long years he was here; nothing prospered with him. When we searched for crystals or flowers he did not find them easily. With difficulty, too, he saw from a distance; he knew not how to arrange the motley lines in order. He broke everything so easily. Yet no other had such craving and ardour to see and hear. Some time back – before the Child was come into our circle – he suddenly became both ready and gay. One day he went out sorrowful. He did not return. Night advanced. We were very anxious on his account. Suddenly, when the glimmer of morning came, we heard his voice in a coppice near. He sang a noble, joyous song. We all marvelled. The Master gazed with rapture towards the dawn as I shall never see him gaze again. After a while the singer came among us, bringing with an expression of ineffable bliss upon his countenance, a dull little Stone of curious shape. The Master took it in his hand and kissed his disciple long; then he looked at us with moist eyes and laid the Stone in an empty place among the other pebbles, just at the point where many lines converged. Never shall I forget that moment. It was as though we had transitorily caught into our souls a clear vision of this wondrous world.

I too am less ready than the others, and Nature seems little disposed to have her treasures found by me. Yet the Master is indulgent to me, and allows me to sit in meditation while the others sally out in research. But it has never been with me as with the Master. All things lead me back upon myself. I well understood what the second Voice said once. I rejoice in the wonderful collections and figures in the study halls; it seems to me as though they were only symbols, veils, decorations enshrouding a Divine Being; and this is ever in my thoughts. I do not seek for them, but I often seek in them. It is as though they might show me the path to a place where, slumbering, lies the Virgin for whom my spirit yearns. The Master has never spoken of this, and I can confide nothing of it to him; it seems to me an inviolable secret. Gladly would I have questioned that child; there was affinity in his bearing, and everything within me seemed illumined by his presence. Had he stayed longer I should certainly have had further experiences. And perhaps even at last my breast might have been unburdened and my tongue freed. Willingly would I have gone with him. But it was not to be. How much longer I shall stay here I know not. It seems as though I should remain for ever. I scarcely dare to admit it to myself, but the conviction forces itself only too deeply upon me. One day I shall find here that which incessantly agitates me; she is immanent. When I go about here in this belief everything endues a higher semblance, a new order, and all is directed toward One Goal. Each object then becomes to me so intimate, so dear, and what yet appears to me as curious and strange suddenly becomes like a household word. Just this strangeness is strange to me, and therefore this Synthesis has always both attracted and repelled me. I cannot and may not understand the Master. He is so incomprehensibly dear to me. He understands me, I know it. He has never spoken against my feelings and my wish. Rather does he desire that each shall follow his own path, because each new path passes through new lands and each eventually leads us back to these Dwellings and to this blessed Hearth. So I too will describe my Figure, and though no mortal lift the veil according to that Inscription, we must seek to become immortal. He who will not lift the veil is no true Disciple at Sais.

NATURE

It must have been long before it occurred to men to describe the manifold objects of their consciousness by a common name, and to set themselves in antithesis thereto. Development is promoted by exercise, and in all development there are divisions, dismemberments that may fitly be compared with the refraction of light rays. Thus it is only gradually that our inner Being has split up into manifold activities, and these divisions may be multiplied through continual exercise. Maybe it is but the morbid disposition of modern men that causes them to lose the power of mingling once more the scattered colours of their soul, and of renewing at will the old simple Nature-condition, and of bringing into effect new and varied combinations. The more united men are in themselves, the more unitedly, the more fully does each phenomenon of Nature strike them. For the nature of the Thought corresponds to the nature of the Impression. And, therefore, to those earlier men everything must have appeared human, familiar and genial. The newest form of Differentiation must have been reflected in their faces; their outward aspect was a true rendering of Nature, and their notions of things must have corresponded with the surrounding world, and have represented a true outlook upon it. Hence it is possible for us to accurately record the thoughts of our ancestors concerning the Universe, and to treat them as important contributions towards a presentation of the terrestrial Nature of that time; particularly from them, as from instruments most proper for the observation of the Universe, we may win a precise account of its Capital Relations, of its relations to its inhabitants and of its inhabitants to it. We find it is just the loftiest questions that first occupied their attention, and that they sought the key to this marvellous Construction either in a Conglomeration of Realities or in the fabled Objectivity of their own unexplained intelligences. It is remarkable that the common foreshadowing of their ideas is to be detected in fluidity, subtleties, formlessness. Well might the inertness and impotence of Matter induce the not insignificant belief in its dependence and inferiority. Early enough some brooding head struck the difficulty of elucidating Form from the formless Forces and Seas. He sought to unravel the tangle by a species of amalgamation, in which process he conceived of the Beginning of Things as minute definitely formed bodies which he apprehended as beyond all imagination small. And he thought it possible to achieve, though not without the help of co-operating intelligences, of attractive and repellent forces, the construction of this monstrous Edifice out of this Sea of Atoms. Still earlier, instead of scientific explanations, we find fairy tales and poems full of

★ 21

amazing picturesque traits in which men, gods and animals are described as co-workers, and we hear the Origin of the World described in the most natural manner. One gains at least the certainty of its fortuitous mechanical Origin, and this presentation of it is significant even to those who scorn the lawless creations of the imagination. To treat the History of the World as the history of Mankind, and to discover only human concerns and relations at every turn is a continuous idea salient through the most different ages and under the most diverse guises, seeming invariably to have held pre-eminence by reason of its prodigious efficacy and its force of easy persuasion. Haphazard Nature herself seems to foster the idea of human personality, and is thus most readily comprehensible as a human being. Hence it is that Poesy is the favourite instrument of the true friend of Nature, and in Poesy the Soul of Nature has ever shone forth most clearly. When one reads and hears true poetry one feels an intimate knowledge of Nature stirring within one, and one floats in it and over it like its own ethereal body. Natural Philosophers and Poets by force of their identical speech have always seemed to be of one race. What the former collected and presented in great ordered masses, the latter kneaded into a daily nourishment for human hearts, splitting up vast Nature and giving it to us in many small convenient portions. While the latter deliriously pursued the Fluent and Fleeting, the former sought with keen knives to detect the inner construction and the inter-relatedness of sinew and muscle. Nature the Friend died under their hands, and left but dead or palpitating remains. While through the Poet, as though moved by generous wine yet still more inspired, she gave forth the most divine and joyous utterances. Uplifted above her quotidian toil she rose to Heaven, danced and prophesied, hailed every guest welcome, and squandered her treasures of glad courage. On this wise she enjoyed heavenly hours with the Poet, and welcomed the Philosopher only when she felt ill or conscience-stricken. Then she gave answer to every question and willingly respected the grave, strong man. Whosoever wills to be well acquainted with her Soul must seek her company with the Poet, for to him she is expansive and pours out her miraculous heart. But whosoever loves her not from the bottom of his heart, and only strives to admire and know her in this or that particular, must go to her sick-room and diligently visit her charnel-house.

We stand in as many incomprehensibly diverse relations towards Nature as towards Man, and as she shows herself childlike to the child, and graciously nestles in his childish heart, so she shows herself to the Gods as divine and in harmony with their great spirits. We cannot assert that Nature exists without asserting something transcendent, and all effort towards the truth in discussion and talk of Nature only leads us further and further from Naturalness. Much is already gained when the endeavour thoroughly to understand Nature rises to a yearning, a tender discreet yearning pleasing to that strange cold Being, if only she be assured of intimate communion. It is a mysterious impulse of our inner being to expand towards all sides from an infinitely deep central point. We believe, when wonderful conscious and unconscious Nature surrounds us, that this impulse is the attraction of Nature, an externalisation of our sympathy with her. But still we seek behind these distant azure forms for home, for the beloved of our youth, parents and brethren, old friends, dear bygone days. Some think that on the Far Side unknown splendours await them, they believe that a vital future is hidden there, and they stretch out their hands in longing towards a New World. Few remain tranquilly among these august surroundings seeking to apprehend them only in their integrity and aggregation. Few there are who in the disunity of the parts do not forget the scintillating filament that connects those parts successively and forms the sacred Lustre, and few there are who feel themselves inspired in the contemplation of this Living Treasure that floats over the Abysses of Night.

Thus originate many and various views of Nature. And if to any the aim in exploring Nature is a merry raid, a feast, yet we see that she changes to a devout religion, imparting to a whole life, guidance, stability, meaning. Already among the primitive nations there were serious spirits for whom Nature was the Face of Divinity; while others, jovial hearts, only invited her to feast. The air was to them as a refreshing draught, the stars were but as torches for the nocturnal dance, and plants and animals nought but costly viands. And so Nature seemed to them not a silent wondrous Temple, but a cheery kitchen and dining-hall. Among these were other and more contemplative souls, who only saw in existing Nature vast unreclaimed alluvion, and they were busy day and night in creating representations of a nobler Nature. They shared the great work sociably.

Some sought to awaken the mute lost notes of the wind and the woods; others expressed their ideas of a more beauteous race in metals and stones; re-arranged the more handsome stones into dwellings; brought to light the treasures hidden in the caverns of the earth; tamed the raging streams, peopled the inhospitable Sea, brought back to the barren zones the old select plants and animals, stemmed the overgrowth of forests and cultivated the finest sorts of flowers and herbs: laid the earth open to the vitalising action of the engendering air and the quickening light; taught the colours how to mingle and arrange themselves in entrancing pictures, and the woods and meadows, springs, and rocks to group themselves once more into lovely gardens; breathed melodies into living limbs in order to awaken them and move them to joyous rhythms; adopted all such poor neglected animals as were susceptible of their control, and purged the woods of noisome monsters, abortions of a degenerate phantasy. Nature soon resumed her more friendly habits, she became more kind and more comfortable, and showed herself willing to be used for the furthering of human ends. Little by little her heart inclined to human ways, her phantasies became more gay, she became more accessible, and willingly answered friendly interrogations. And thus little by little the antique Golden Age seemed to come again, in which she was the Friend, Consoler, Priestess, and Miracle-worker to Humanity, when she lived among them, and Man through heavenly communion became Immortal.

Then will the Stars again visit the Earth with whom they were wroth in the days of Her darkening; then the Sun will lay down his mighty sway and become again a star among other stars, and all the

Nations of the World will meet together once more after long separation. Then the old alienated families will find each other and every day shall witness new greetings, new embraces; then will the ancient inhabitants of the Earth return to her, on every hill the ashes will kindle anew, everywhere the flames of life will blaze high, old habitations will be rebuilt, ancient times will be renewed, and history will become the dream of an infinite everlasting Now.

Whoever is of this stock, of this Faith, and whoever will participate in this civilising of Nature should go into the studio of the artist, should hearken everywhere to the unguessed ever-emergent poetry. He must never be tired of observing Nature or of accompanying her; he must follow the indications of her finger, and spare himself no tedious journey if she beckon him. He must spurn no wearisome course. Even were he to go through dark caverns he will certainly find fabulous treasure; the miner's little lamp burns steady at the far end, and who knows to what Divine Mysteries an enchanting inhabitant of the Kingdoms of the Under World may not initiate him.

None, surely, wanders further from the goal than he who imagines that he already knows the marvellous Kingdom and that he can in a few words fathom its constitution and find the right path everywhere. To no one who has torn himself loose and made himself into an island does insight come of itself nor yet without pain. This can only happen to children or to men who are childlike and know not what they do. Long unremitting intercourse, free and curious contemplation, attention to faint tokens and indications, an inward poet life, practised senses, a simple God-fearing spirit, these are the essential requisites of a true friend of Nature, without which none will attain his wish. It does not seem sensible to attempt to comprehend and understand a human World without ourself possessing a fully developed Humanity. Not one of the senses may slumber, and if all are not equally awake, each one must be excited and not allowed to languish or be stifled. Just as we discern the future painter in the boy who covers all the walls and every flat space with drawings, and variedly combines colour with design, so we see an incipient Philosopher in him who without pause investigates all natural

★ 25

objects, questions, takes heed to all, brings together whatever is remarkable, and rejoices if he become Master and Possessor of a new phenomenon, a new strength and knowledge.

To some, it seems not worth while to pursue the endless subdivisions of Nature and that moreover it is a dangerous undertaking, unproductive of fruit or result. As we can never find the ultimate atom of material bodies, never find their simplest cell because magnitudes lose themselves forwards and backwards in infinity, so likewise is it with the species of bodies and forces. Among them we chance everlastingly on new species, new combinations, new phenomena. These only seem to be arrested when our zeal slackens. And so we waste our precious time in vapid contemplation and tedious enumeration, till this becomes at last a real delirium, a confirmed vertigo in face of the appalling abyss. For so far as Man has come Nature remains always the awful Mill of Death. Everywhere monstrous Revolution, unaccountable Vortices. It is a sovereignty of Rapine, of maddest Wantonness, an Immensity pregnant with Woe. The few luminous points only reveal a yet more horrid Night, and terrors of all sorts paralyse each observer. Death stands like a Saviour beside piteous Humanity; for without Death the Maddest were the Happiest. And it is just the effort to fathom this gigantic Mechanism that is in itself an impulse toward the Abyss, a commencing vertigo. For every enticement is a growing whorl which soon overpowers the unhappy one, and at last whirls him away through a terrific Night. Here are the pitfalls deep laid against human understanding that Nature is ever seeking to annihilate everywhere as her greatest enemy. Blessed are the childlike innocence and ignorance of men which have kept them unaware of the gruesome dangers which hang like fearful thunderclouds over their peaceful abodes and are prepared to break upon them at any moment. Only the dissension of the forces of Nature has so far preserved man. Nevertheless the great moment cannot tarry in which the assembled races of man by a great common resolve will tear themselves from this sorrowful plight, from this galling bondage, and when by a voluntary renunciation of their present possessions they will emancipate their kind for ever from this Woe, and will lead them in a happier world back to their ancient Father.

So might they end worthily and prevent their necessary and violent annihilation or a still more atrocious degeneration into beasts by progressive deterioration of their mental faculties, through insanity.

Association with the forces of Nature, with animals, plants, rocks, stones and waves must of necessity mould man to a resemblance to these objects. And this resemblance, this metamorphosis, this flux of divine and human in indomitable forces is the very Spirit of Nature, that terrible engulfing power. And is not all that we see already plunder from Heaven, the immense Ruin of former Glories, the Remains of an abominable Repast?

Good! say the more courageous! Let our race maintain a lengthy well-pondered war of destruction with this Nature. With slow insidious poisons we must seek to overcome her. The Natural Philosopher may be a noble hero who hurls himself into the yawning abyss to save his fellow-men. The artists have played her many a secret prank. Go on in the same way, get possession of the mystic threads and make her to war against her own members. Make use of every discord that you may lead her according to your pleasure like that fire-breathing Bull. She must be in subjection to you. Patience and Faith become the Children of Men. Distant brothers are united with us in one Endeavour. The Wheel of the Stars will become the Spinning Wheel of our Life Thread and then our slaves shall build us a new Land. Let us gaze on her tumult and her devastations with inward triumph. She shall sell herself to us and for every deed of violence she shall pay a heavy penalty. Let us live and die in the inspiring sentiment of our Freedom, for herein the stream rises that shall one day submerge and tame her. In it let us bathe and refresh ourselves to new deeds of heroism. The Monster's rage reaches not hither; one little drop of Freedom is enough to cripple her forever and to set a limit and a term to her ravages."

"They are right," cry several. "Here or nowhere lies the Talisman. We sit at the Source of Freedom and look out from thence. This is the great Magic Mirror in which all creation wholly and clearly

★ 27

images itself, in it do the tender spirits and forms of all natures bathe. Here every chamber is unlocked. What does it profit wearily to plod round the grim world of visible objects? The veritable world lies within us, in this source. Here is revealed the true meaning of this great motley crazy Show, and if full of this revelation we traverse Nature again, everything appears familiar and with assurance we distinguish every form. We do not need to investigate at length; a slight resemblance, a few indications in the sand are enough to inform us. Everything becomes a great Script to which we have the key; nothing is unexpected because we anticipate the evolution of the great Time Machine. We only enjoy Nature in the plenitude of our senses because she does not divide us from them, because no fever dreams oppress us and a clear recollection renders us serene and confident."

"The others rave," said a serious man to these last. "Do they not recognise in Nature a true image of themselves? They consume themselves in a savage nescience. They do not know that their Nature is a conjuration of their thought, a barren phantasy of their dream. Of course to them she is a hideous beast, a strange extravagant masque of their own greed. The awakened Man sees this spawn of his disordered imagination without a shudder, for he knows it is but the futile spectre of his own weakness. He feels himself Master of the World, his Ego soars mightily over the Abyss and will soar through eternities of endless vicissitude. His inward spirit strives to proclaim and promote unison. Through the endless ages he will be ever more and more united with himself and the creation that surrounds him, and he will see standing out more clearly his higher Ego, the eternal All Efficiency of a high moral World-Order.

"Reason is the meaning of the World. The World exists because of it, and if at first it is the battle-ground of a child-like budding Reason it will one day become the divine image of its activity, the theatre of a true Church. Until such time let man honour it as the emblem of his spirit, the emblem that will ennoble itself together with him by indeterminate degrees. Whosoever wills to attain to a knowledge of Nature must exercise his moral sense, must fashion and mould the noble core of his inmost Being to the measure of moral order, and Nature will, as if of her own choice, lay herself bare before him. Moral action is the only and great experiment in which are solved all the riddles of manifold phenomena. Whoever grasps this Moral Order and is able to analyse it in strict logical sequence is forever Master of Nature."

The Disciple listens to these conflicting voices with dismay. Each one seems to him to be right, and a strange perplexity takes possession of his soul. Gradually the inward commotion subsides, and over the murky internecine waves a Spirit of Peace seems to hover, whose approach is heralded in the youth's soul by a new courage and a convincing joy.

A merry playfellow, his temples decked with roses and convolvulus came running by and saw him sitting absorbed in himself. "Dreamer!" he cried, "thou art quite on the wrong road. In such a way thou wilt make no great progress. The mood's the best of all things. Is that indeed a mood of Nature? Thou art still young, and dost thou not feel the dictates of youth in every vein? Do not Love and Longing fill thy breast? How canst thou sit in solitude? Does Nature sit solitary? Joy and desire flee from the solitary; and what use is Nature to thee without desire? Only with men is she at home, this Spirit who crowds all the senses with a thousand different colours, who surrounds thee like an invisible Lover. At our Feasts her tongue is loosed; she sits aloft and carols songs of gladdest life. Thou hast never yet loved, poor fellow; at the first kiss a new world will open to thee and life will penetrate thy ravished heart with its thousand rays. I will tell thee a tale. Listen! There lived once upon a time in the land of the setting sun a young man. He was very good, but above the ordinary extraordinary. He fretted himself incessantly about nothing and yet again nothing, went quietly about on his own account when others played together and were merry, and indulged in strange things. Caves and woods were his favourite haunts; he talked continually with quadrupeds and birds, with trees and rocks; of course in no sensible words, but only in such foolish twaddle as would make one die of laughing. But he ever remained morose and solemn notwithstanding that the squirrels and monkeys, the parrots and bullfinches gave themselves all the trouble in the world to distract him and put him in the right path again. The goose told him tales, the stream rippled a roundelay, a great heavy stone made comic leaps and a rose crept round him amicably and twined herself in his locks, while the ivy caressed his thoughtful brow. But his solemnity and depression were stubborn. His parents were very grieved; they knew not what they ought to do. He was healthy and eat well; they had never crossed him. Only a few years back he was cheerful and blithe as anyone, first in all games, and approved by every maiden. He was really beautiful, looked like a picture and danced like an angel. Amongst the maidens there was one, a precious, exquisite child; she seemed to be of wax, her hair was like gold silk, her lips were cherry red like a doll's, her eyes burning black. Who saw her might have thought to perish of it, so lovely was she. At that time Rosenbllitchen, for so she was called, was dear to the beautiful Hyacinth, for that was his name, and in fact he loved her to the point of death. The other children knew nothing about it. The violet had whispered it to them first. The house kittens had noticed it, for the houses of their parents lay close together. When at night Hyacinth stood at his window and Rosenbliitchen at hers, and the little cats passed by on their mouse-hunt and saw the two there they laughed and giggled so loud that it made the lovers quite cross. The violet had told it in confidence to the strawberry, who told it to her friend the gooseberry, who did not omit to scratch Hyacinth as he came along. So very soon the whole garden and wood knew all about it, and when Hyacinth went out there rang from all sides: "Little Rosen-blutchen is my darling!" Then Hyacinth was annoyed, but he had to laugh with all his heart when a little lizard came gliding past, sat himself on a warm stone, and waving his little tail, sang: –

Rosenbliitchen, little pet,
Once upon a time went blind,
So when Hyacinth she met
She embraced him. Being blind
She just thought he was her mother,

When she found it was another
Did she mind? no not a bit,
Only kissed him as before.
Was she frightened? not a whit,
Merely kissed him more and more.

Alas, how soon this glorious time was over. There came a man from foreign parts who had travelled astonishingly far, who had a long beard, deep eyes, fearsome eyebrows, and who wore a marvellous robe of many folds with strange figures woven into it. He sat himself down before the house belonging to Hyacinth's parents. Hyacinth was filled with curiosity, and went out to him and brought him bread and wine. He parted his white beard, and told his story far on into the night. Hyacinth kept awake and did not fidget nor grow tired of listening. From what transpired afterwards he told a great deal about strange lands, of unexplored regions, of amazing extraordinary things. He stayed there three days and descended with Hyacinth into profound depths. Rosenbliitchen heartily cursed the old warlock, for Hyacinth became quite possessed by his discourse, and concerned himself with nothing else. He would scarcely take his food. At last the old man went away, but he left with Hyacinth a little book in which no one could read. Hyacinth gave him more fruit, bread and wine, and accompanied him far upon his way. He returned pensive and from thenceforward began a new way of life. Rosenbliitchen certainly had a right to be pitied for from that time he made little enough of her, and was always self-engrossed. Now it happened that one day he came home, and was as though new born. He fell on the necks of his parents and wept. "I must away into strange lands," he said; "the old Sibyl in the forest has told me how I am to become whole; she threw the book into the fire, and bade me come to you and ask your blessing. Perhaps I may return soon, perhaps never. Greet little Rosenbliitchen; I would willingly have spoken with her. I know not how it is with me; something urges me away. If I try to think of the old days, mightier thoughts intervene. Peace is fled together with heart and love. I must go seek them. I would like to tell you whither, but I do not know. Thither where the

Mother of All Things lives, the Veiled Virgin. My desire is aflame for Her. Farewell." He tore himself away from them and departed. His parents lamented and shed tears. Rosenbliitchen stayed in her chamber and wept bitterly. Hyacinth hastened through valleys and deserts, over mountains and streams, towards the Mysterious Land. He questioned men and animals, rocks and trees concerning Isis, the sacred Goddess. Many laughed, many kept silence, from none did he receive the information he sought. At first he passed through a rude wild country; mists and clouds intercepted his passage and never-ceasing storms. Then he passed through interminable deserts of sand and fiery dust, and as he wandered his humour also was changed. The time seemed long to him; the inward tumult was appeased, he grew more gentle and the mighty urgence was gradually reduced to a quiet but intense aspiration in which his whole spirit was melted. It was as though many years had passed over him. The country became at the same time richer and more varied, the air warm and azure, the road more level. Green bushes allured him with pleasant shade. But he did not understand their speech. Besides they did not seem to speak while yet they filled his heart with green colours and a cool still perfume. That sweet longing waxed higher and higher in him, and the leaves expanded with sap; birds and beasts were noisier and more joyous, the fruits more aromatic, the heavens a deeper blue, the air milder, his love warmer, time went faster as if it saw itself nearing the goal. One day he lighted on a crystal brook, and on a cloud of flowers that came tripping down the valley between black mountain peaks as high as heaven. They greeted him kindly, with familiar words. "Dear country folk," he said, "where can I really find the sacred dwelling-place of Isis? It must needs be somewhere near here, and you are perhaps more at home than I." "We are only passing through," answered the flowers; "a family of spirits is travelling abroad, and we prepare their way and resting-place. Yet we have but just come through a place where we heard your name. Only go upwards whence we came, and you will learn more." The flowers and the brook laughed as they said this, offered him a refreshing draught, and went on their way. He followed their advice, asked again and again, and finally came to that long-sought dwelling that lay hidden beneath palms and other rare trees. His heart beat with an infinite yearning, and the sweetest shyness overcame him in this habitation of the eternal centuries. He slumbered enveloped by heavenly perfumes, for it was only a dream that could lead him to the Holy of Holies. Mysteriously his dream led him to the sound of loud, delicious music and alternating harmonies through endless halls full of curious things. It all seemed to him so familiar, and yet of an hitherto unrecognised splendour. Then the last vestiges of earthliness disappeared as though consumed in air, and he stood before the Celestial Virgin. He raised the diaphanous glistening veil, and Rosenbliitchen sank into his arms. A distant music encompassed the secrets of the lovers' meeting, and the effusions of their love, and shut away everything inharmonious from this abode of rapture. Hyacinth lived ever after with Rosenbliitchen, among his glad parents and his playfellows, and innumerable grandchildren thanked the old Sibyl for her counsel and her fire, for at that time people had as many children as they wished for.

The Disciples embraced each other and separated. The wide echoing Halls stood empty and deserted, and the marvellous Conversation between the thousand natural objects collected together in these halls and set out in many fashioned orders, proceeded in countless accents. The different Forces sported together. They strove once more in their freedom, in their former relationship. A few kept to their proper places, and looked on at the varied movement around them undisturbed. The others complained of their dreadful pains and sufferings, and lamented the old splendid life in the lap of Nature, where a common liberty united them, and each found in himself whatever he needed. "Oh, that man," said they, "understood the hidden music of Nature, and had the sense of external harmonies! But he hardly is aware that we belong together and that no one of us can exist without the other. He can never let anything be. Tyrannically he separates us and gropes about in loud dissonances. How happy could he be if he communed with us kindly, if he entered our great Bond as once he did in the Golden Age, as he so justly terms it. In that Age he understood us as we understood him. His desire to be a god it is that has divided us; he seeks what we can never know nor imagine, and now he is neither a voice accompanying nor a cadence completing us. He anticipates the infinite satisfaction, the everlasting delight there is in us, and that is why he has such an extraordinary love for some among us. The magic of gold, the mystery of colour, the joy of water, are not unknown to him; through the antiques he has a glimpse of the marvels of stone. And yet the sweet passion for the work of Nature is lacking in him, and the eye to see our entrancing mysteries. Could he but learn to feel! Of this divinest, this most natural of all faculties he knows as yet but little; through this faculty the ancient desired Time will come again; the element of this faculty is an inner light that breaks into strong beautiful colours. Then will the stars arise in him; he will learn to feel the whole world more clearly and more variously, while as yet his eyes disclose only lines and surfaces to him. He will be Leader in an endless play of Forces, and will forget all his foolish strivings in an eternal self-subsisting and ever-waxing felicity. Thought is but a dream of sensation, merely dead sensation, pulseless feeble life.

As they spoke thus the sun streamed through the lofty windows, and the noise of the conversation was lost in a soft murmuring. A limitless anticipation thrilled through all those forms, a caressing warmth was diffused over them, and the most marvellous of Nature's songs soared up out of the stillest silence. Voices of men were heard in the vicinity, the great doors on to the garden were flung back, and several wayfarers sat themselves on the steps of the wide stairway in the shadow of the building. In beauteous light before them lay the entrancing landscape, and in the distance sight lost itself among the blue hills. Friendly children brought a variety of viands and drinks, and soon a lively conversation sprang up among them.

"To everything that a man does he must give his undivided attention or his Ego," said one at last. "When he has done this, thoughts soon arise in him, or else a new method of apprehension miraculously appears, which seems to be nothing else than gentle oscillations of a something that colours or resounds, or the marvellous contractions and figurations of an elastic fluid. They radiate with a lively mobility from the side where the impression left its sting, and carry his Ego away. He can often immediately annul this play of Forces if he divide his attention again, or let it ramble capriciously around. For it seems to be nothing but the rays and effects which every Ego sets in motion in all directions through the elastic medium, or it is the diffraction of this very medium, or speaking generally, it is the irregular play of the waves of this sea on the inflexible attention. Very remarkable it is that through this play of his personality man first becomes aware of his specific freedom, and that it seems to him as though he awaked out of a deep sleep, as though he were only now at home in the world and as if the light of day were breaking now over his interior life for the first time. He seems to have brought it to the highest perfection when he is able, without disturbing this same play of Forces, to occupy himself with the ordinary business of the senses, and feel and think at the same time. Both methods of apprehension profit by this. The external world becomes transparent, the interior world multiform and significant. And thus a man finds himself in a condition of relationship between two worlds in completest freedom, plenitude and power. It is natural that a man should seek to eternalise this condition, and to extend it over the whole sum of his impressions, that he should never tire of tracing these associations in both worlds, and of investigating their laws, their sympathies and antipathies. The substance of these impressions which affect us we call Nature, and thus Nature stands in an immediate relationship to those functions of our bodies which we call senses. Unknown and mysterious relations of our body allow us to surmise unknown and mysterious correlations with Nature, and therefore Nature is that wondrous fellowship into which our bodies introduce us, and which we learn to know through the mode of its constitution and abilities.

It is open to question whether we can really learn to know the Nature of Natures through differentiated Nature, and to what degree our thoughts and the intensity of our attention are determined by her or determine her, and whether we in this way break away from Nature, and perhaps pervert her tender compliancy. We see that these inner relationships and constitutions of our body must be examined before all else, before we can hope to answer these questions, or penetrate to the Nature of things. It might also be thought that we ought to be expert reasoners before we attempt to seek the hidden cohesions of our body, or endeavour to employ its intelligence for the understanding of Nature. And then assuredly nothing could be more natural than to practise all possible exercise of thought, and to acquire a proficiency, an ease at this business so as to pass from one subject to another, and to unite and resolve them in diverse ways. To that end we should attentively observe all impressions and likewise note the play of thought thence issuing, and we ought occasionally in this way to experience new thoughts which should also be attended to, so that we may, through frequent practice, learn to distinguish and keep separate the impression from the movements bound up with them. If we had thus obtained only a few movements, as it were an alphabet of Nature, the deciphering would have sped more easily, and the power over thought-creation and activity would set the observer in a position, even without previous true experience, to delineate Nature compositions, and to devise Nature thoughts. And then the Goal were reached.

"It is very hazardous," said another, "to reconstruct Nature from external forces and phenomena, and to declare her now a monstrous Fire, now a wonderfully contrived Accident, now a Duality or Trinity, or some other portentous Force. It were more conceivable she proved the creation of an incomprehensible co-understanding of infinitely different beings, the miraculous link with the world of souls, the point of union and point of contact of numberless worlds."

"It may be hazardous," said a third, "but the more ingeniously woven is the net flung out by the bold fisherman, the luckier is the catch. Only encourage a man to pursue his road as far as possible, and let everyone be welcome who weaves a new phantasy over realities. Thinkest thou not 'twill be from the well worked out systems that the future Geographer of Nature will select the data for his great map of Nature? He will compare them, and the comparison will first inform us concerning the singular country. But the cognition of Nature will differ immensely from our exposition of her. The interpreter proper will perhaps arrive at being able to induce several natural forces to a simultaneous production of more beautiful and more useful phenomena, he will improvise on Nature as on some great instrument, and yet he will not understand Nature. This is the gift of the Historian of Nature, of the Time Seer, who entrusted with the history of Nature, and acquainted with the World, heralds the transcendent scene of Nature-history, apprehending and prophesying her significance.

"This territory is still unexplored, a Holy Land. Celestial ambassadors alone have let a few syllables of this sublime science fall, and it is only surprising that the prescient spirits have neglected these premonitions, and have degraded Nature to the level of a uniform machine without Past or Future. Everything divine has a history, and shall not Nature, the only Unity with which man may compare himself, be, just as well as man, comprised in a history, or, which is the same thing, have a soul? Nature would not be Nature had she no soul, she would not be that unique counterpart of Humanity, not the indispensable Answer to that mystic Question, or the Question to that infinite Answer."

"Only the poets have felt what Nature can be to man," began a lovely youth, "and one may well say that in them Humanity finds its most complete expression, and therefore each impression is transmitted unsullied in all its endless modifications, towards all sides, through the crystal clearness and activity of their spirits. They find everything in Nature. To them alone her soul is not alien, and not vainly do they search in this communion, for all the Beatitudes of the Golden Age. For them Nature has all the variability of a limitless soul, she surprises them more than the most ready and clever man by her ingenious turns and incidents, by her meetings (confluences) and her deviations, by her great ideas and vagaries. Such are the inexhaustible riches of her fancy that no one seeks her companionship in vain. She beautifies everything, she animates and confirms everything, and if occasionally nothing but a senseless unmeaning Machine seems to govern everything, still may the deep seeing eye discern a wondrous sympathy with human hearts in Coincidences, and in the results of simple fortuitous Occurrences. The Wind is a movement of the air which may be the effect of several causes, but is it not something more to the lonely yearning heart when it soughs overhead, wafted from dear lands, does it not seem to transform his silent pain into a deep melodious sigh of Nature? Does not the tender green of a Spring meadow express with charming fidelity the whole flower-decked soul of the young lover, and is the exaltation of any joyous soul steeped in golden wine more precious and exciting than the view of the ripe gleaming cluster of grapes that half conceals itself beneath broad leaves? We accuse poets of exaggeration; we only approve of their unusual language when we can enjoy their fancies about marvellous Nature without deep research. They see and hear many things that others neither see nor hear, and in a sweet frenzy dispose of and make free with the Real World according to their pleasure. But to me it seems the poets do not exaggerate enough by half, that they only guess darkly at the magic of that Speech, and only play with Phantasy as a child plays with his father's divining-rod. They do not know what Forces are subject to them, what words must obey them. For is it not true that stones and forest trees obey music, and, tamed by it, are docile as house dogs? Do not verily the loveliest flowers spring up around the beloved, and do they not rejoice to engarland her? Does not the sky become glad for her, and the sea more tranquil? Does not all Nature, even as the countenance and the gestures, the pulse and the colour express the condition of that superior wonderful Being we call Man? Does not the rock become individual when I address it? And what else am I than the river when I gaze with melancholy in its waves, and my thoughts are lost in its course? Only a serene exuberant spirit can understand the plant world, and animals are only to be known by a merry child or a savage. Whether any one has yet understood the stones or the stars I know not, but such an one must certainly have been a gifted being. In those statues which remain from a bygone time to testify to the

★ 38

beauty of man so profound a spirit shines, so strange an understanding of the stone world, that the contemplative observer seems enclosed in a contracting stony rind. The Sublime petrifies, and therefore we ought not to marvel at the Sublime in Nature and at its effects, or be ignorant of where to seek it. Might not Nature have turned to stone before the glance of God? Or from terror at the advent of Man?"

He who had just spoken was plunged in meditation during this discourse. The distant mountains were dyed in the after-glow, and evening descended over the landscape with sweet trustfulness. After a long pause he was heard to say: "To understand Nature we must let Nature evolve herself to the fullest in us. For this enterprise we must make up our mind to be determined solely by divine aspirations towards beings that resemble us, and to distinguish their essential characteristics. For verily all Nature is only comprehensible as the instrument and medium of the intelligence of a reasonable Being. A thoughtful man turns to the primary functions of his being, to the creative speculation, back to the point where production and knowledge exist together in the most wonderful state of flux, to that generative moment of peculiar bliss, of inward auto-conception. If he be absolutely sunk in the contemplation of this original phenomenon there spreads out before him, like some unlimited pageant of rising seasons and places, a history of Nature's evolution, and each point that establishes itself in the boundless fluidity will be a new revelation to him of the Genius of Love, a new volume of the Thou and the I. The punctilious description of this inner world history is the true theory of Nature. Through the inter-coherence of his own world of thought and its harmony with the universe, a system of thought arises spontaneously as the true image and formula of the Universe. But the art of peaceful Meditation, of generative cosmic speculation is difficult. The undertaking is furthered by incessant reflection, by a severe austerity, and its satisfaction will be not the applause of contemporaries who shrink from fatigue, but only the joy of knowledge and growth, an inner rhythm with the Universe."

"Yes," answered the second, "nothing is so remarkable as the great simultaneity of Nature. She seems to be present in her fulness throughout. All the forces of Nature are active in the flame of a light; she represents and transforms herself perpetually everywhere. She drives leaves, flowers and fruits together, and in the midst of Time is at once Past, Present and Future. And who knows in what singular sort she may be also working from the distance, or whether our system of Nature be only a sun in the Universe, linked to it by bonds through one light, one attraction and one influence, which things will presently reveal themselves to our spirit, out of which we shall then pour the spirit of the Universe over this very Nature, and shall participate the spirit of this Nature with further Nature systems. When the Thinker, said a third, treads the strenuous path as Adept, and seeks by a skilful application of his spiritual activities to reduce the Sum of Things to a simple enigmatic Figure, one might say 'Nature dances,' and when he describes in words the curves of her movements the Lover of Nature must admire this audacious undertaking, and rejoice too at the success of this human enterprise. The Adept reasonably esteems action highly. His existence is Action and Production by Knowledge and "Will, and his Art consists in applying his tools to everything, in representing the world in his fashion. Hence the principle of his world is Action, and his world is his Art. Here again Nature is manifest in a new splendour, and only the thoughtless man throws aside the indecipherable wonderful chaotic Words with scorn. Thankfully the Priest lays this new sublime Geometry on the altar by the side of the magnetic needle that has never erred, and that has brought back numberless ships over the pathless ocean to the inhabited shores and the harbours of the Fatherland. Beside the thinkers there are yet other friends to Knowledge who do not succeed in bringing forth their thoughts, and who, though without vocation for this Art, become beloved pupils of Nature, their joy being found in learning, not in teaching; in experience, not in action; in receiving, not in giving. Some are diligent and confident of the omnipresence and intimate inter-relationship of Nature, and convinced in advance of the defectiveness and persistence of the individual phenomena, select some one phenomenon with care, and fix fast its principle under its thousand changing forms with steady gaze; and holding to this clue they explore every cranny of the secret laboratory in order to trace a complete plan of its labyrinthine passages. When they have done with this fatiguing work, all unnoticed a loftier spirit possesses them, and it is easy to them to speak of the Chart that lies before them, and to point out the path to every inquirer. Invaluable utility hallows their arduous work, and the grand plan of their Chart will accord with the System of the Thinker in a quite surprising manner; and to their consolation they will have led him to the living Demonstration of his abstract Theories. Like children, the idlest among them await the benevolent communication of the science of Nature which is necessary to them from some nobler Being who is fervently adored by them. In this so short life they had rather not devote time and attention to business cut off from the service of Love. By pious behaviour they but seek to win Love, to share Love untroubled by the great display of Forces, tranquilly to surrender their destinies to this Realm of Power because they are filled with the inward conviction of their inseparability from the Beloved Being, and Nature only moves them as Her image and Her possession. Why do their happy souls seek to know? They have chosen the better part, and only glow like pure flames of Love in this terrestrial world on the pinnacles of Temples and on the masts of the wandering ships, witnessing to the overflowing celestial Fire. Often, in sacred hours, these loving children learn beautiful things from out the secrets of Nature, and in their ignorant simplicity are bold with her. The investigator follows in their footsteps in order to collect every bauble which they in their innocence and joy have let drop. Their love graces the sympathising Poet who seeks to propagate in other times and other lands this very Love, this Seed from the Golden Altar." "Oh! whose heart is not stirred with tumultuous joy when the intimate Life of Nature enters into his soul in all its plenitude," cried a youth with flashing eyes, "when that mighty sentiment for which language has no other name than Love is diffused in him, like some powerful all-dissolving vapour, when he, shivering with sweet terror, sinks into the dusky,

★ 41

enticing bosom of Nature, when the meagre personality loses itself in the over-powering waves of passion, and nothing remains but the focal point of the incommensurable generative Force, an engulfing vortex in the ocean? What is this universally emergent flame? A mystic embrace whose sweet fruit sheds itself in precious drops as dew. Water, that first-born child of aërial Fusion, cannot deny his voluptuous origin, and with celestial dominance shows himself the element of Love's union on the earth. Not without truth have the Ancient Sages sought the origin of things in Water; and, in truth, they have spoken of a more imperishable Water than seas and springs. In that is revealed the original Flux, such as is manifest in fused metals, and therefore men should ever honour it as divine. How few as yet have steeped themselves in the secrets of Fluidity, and in the intoxicated soul of many this anticipation of highest bliss and life has never arisen. The Soul of the world reveals itself in this mighty yearning toward Liquefaction. The drunken feel only too well this supernatural rapture of Fluidity, and finally all our pleasant sensations are different liquefactions, movements of this original fluid in us. Sleep itself is nothing but the Flowing of the invisible Sea, and awakening but the Turn of the Tide. How many men stand by the brink of the intoxicating floods and do not hear the lullaby of the maternal waters, and do not enjoy the entrancing play of their infinite waves. In the Golden Age we lived like these waves, in multi-coloured clouds, in shimmering seas, and living waters of earth loved and revealed themselves to the races of mankind in eternal play. They were visited by the Children of Heaven, and it was only in that great catastrophe called by Holy Writ the Flood that this flourishing world was submerged. A hostile Being cast down the Earth, and but a few men remained floating on the summits of the mountains of an alien world. How strange that just the most sacred and most adorable phenomena of Nature are in the hands of such moribund men as the chemists seem to be! they who puissantly awaken the generative consciousness of Nature, which should be only the secret of Lovers, mysteries of the higher Humanity. These things are thoughtlessly and shamelessly provoked by coarse natures, who will never know what

★ 42

marvels surround their lens. Only Poets should commune with fluidity, and only ardent youth shall tell of it. Laboratories would become Temples, and Mankind would honour and celebrate their flames and their liquids with a new love. How happy, then, would those cities esteem themselves which are watered by the sea or by a great river! And each spring would become again the commonwealth of Love and the abode of learned and spiritual men. It is because of this nothing so entices children as fire and water; every stream promises to lead them to the iridescent horizon, to lovelier regions. It is not only a reflection of Heaven that lies in the water, it is a tender befriending, a symbol of neighbourliness; and if the unappeased desire strives after the illimitable heights, then Love content sinks to the bottomless deep. But it is vain to attempt to teach and preach Nature. One born blind does not learn to see though we tell him for ever about colours, lights, and distant forms. Just so no one will understand Nature who has not the necessary organ, the inward instrument, the specific creating instrument, no one who does not as if spontaneously recognise and distinguish Nature everywhere in all things, nor one who does not with an inherent lust of Creation mingle himself by means of Sensation in manifold relationship with all bodies, and feel his way into them simultaneously. Whosoever has a proper and practised sense of Nature enjoys Nature, while as he studies her and rejoices in her infinite complexity, in the inexhaustibility of her delights, desires that we trouble him not with unnecessary words. Rather it seems to him Nature cannot be treated with too much secrecy, cannot be too tenderly spoken of, cannot be observed too calmly or too attentively. With her he feels as in the bosom of a chaste bride, and even such an one he trusts only in the sweetest most confidential moments with the knowledge he has attained. Happy I esteem this Son, this Favourite of Nature, to whom she permits a vision of herself in her Duality as an engendering and a conceiving Force, and in her Unity as an infinite everlasting Hymen. His life will be the fulness of all joys, a chain of well-being, and his religion will be the one real Naturalism."

During this conversation the Master and his Disciples had

approached the company. The travellers stood up and greeted him respectfully. A refreshing coolness was exhaled from the dark shrubberies over the terrace and stairway. The Master commanded a rare glowing Stone should be brought, the one that is called carbuncle, and a potent ruddy light streamed over the different faces and costumes. Soon a friendly sympathy was established among them. While a distant music sounded, the strangers recounted the remarkable reminiscences of their wide travels, and a cool flame from crystal vessels flowed into the mouths of the speakers. They had set out full of yearning and curiosity to seek traces of the bygone antique peoples of whom existing men seem but the degenerate and brutalised descendants, and whose high civilisation we have to thank for the most momentous and indispensable knowledge and instruments. Especially had the sacred tongue attracted them, which was once the resplendent link between the Royal Men and the Supernatural Regions and their inhabitants, and of which some few Words had remained, according to the report of many legends in the possession of some happy sages among our ancestors. Its enunciation was a miraculous chant whose sounds penetrated deep into the core of each Nature and analysed it. Each of its names seems the word of deliverance for the Soul of each natural Body. These vibrations evoked with generative force images of world phenomena, and one could say of them with truth that the life of the Universe was an eternal thousand-tongued discourse. For in these words all energies, all species of Activity, seemed to be united most incomprehensibly. To search for fragments of this language, or at least for some information concerning it had been the main object of their journey, and the call of Antiquity had led them to Sais. Here they hoped to obtain important information from the learned Guardians of the Temple archives, and perhaps to find an elucidation in the large collections of every kind. They begged permission of the Master to sleep one night in the Temple, and to attend his lectures for a few days. They were accorded what they asked, and they rejoiced inwardly to see how the Master accompanied their stories with many comments drawn from the treasures of his experience, and how he unfolded to them a wealth of instructive and agreeable anecdote and description. He spoke at last of the business of his age in awakening the different senses of Nature in youthful minds, of practising and sharpening them, and of joining them to other aptitudes so as to bring forth flowers and fruit. To be Herald of Nature is a beautiful and holy Mission, said the Master. But it is not enough to possess the totality and continuity of information, not enough the gift of knitting this information easily and clearly to things already known and experienced, or to interchange peculiar-sounding words with commonly-used expressions, not enough the agility of a rich imagination to arrange the phenomena of Nature in easily intelligible and strikingly illuminated pictures that either by the charm of composition or the riches of their contents invigorate and satisfy the senses or ravish the spirit by their profound significance. None of these things are the true requisites of a Herald of Nature. For those for whom there is something else to do than to associate with Nature these things are perhaps enough, but whoso detects in himself an inward yearning towards Nature, whoso seeks for all satisfaction in her, and is as it were a sentient instrument of her secret activities, he will only recognise as Master and as Confidant of Nature him who speaks of her with gravity and faith, whose speech has the marvellous, inimitable impressiveness and individuality that announces true gospel, true inspiration. The favourable original dispositions of such a natural intelligence must be fostered with untiring zeal from earliest days by silence and solitude because much talking is incompatible with the fixed attention that such an one must exercise; it must also be built up and strengthened by a simple and discreet life and unwearying patience. It is impossible to predetermine the length of time in which her secrets are communicated. Some lucky ones succeed in obtaining them early, others only at an advanced age. A true seeker never becomes old, every Eternal Quest is outside the bonds of Life, and the more the outer husk withers, the clearer, the brighter, the more potently glows the kernel. And this gift does not depend upon outward beauty or strength or insight, or any other human prerogative. In all conditions, among all ages and races, in every epoch, under all latitudes, there have been men whom Nature has chosen as her favourites, and who have been gladdened by an inner receptivity. Often these men have seemed more artless and unskilful than others, and remain all their lives in the obscurity of the great multitude. It should be regarded as a rare occurrence to find a true understanding of Nature united to great eloquence, prudence and a splendid bearing, for it usually accompanies or produces a simple speech, wisdom and an unpretentious life. In the workshop of the artist and the artisan, and wherever man is in complex relations and in strife with Nature, as in agriculture, in navigation, in cattle-breeding, in mining and in many other industries, the development of this sense seems to take place most easily and often. If all art consists in acquaintance with the means of attaining a desired goal, of producing a predetermined effect or phenomenon, in the ability to choose and employ these means, then, those who feel the inward call to make the understanding of Nature shared by a greater number of men, and to develop and cultivate those aptitudes assiduously in men, must first carefully regard the natural occasions of this development, and seek to learn the fundamental principles of this art of Nature. With the help of this acquired insight a system for the employment of these means will be formed on experiment, comparison and analysis for each several individual who will familiarise himself with this system until it is like a second nature to him, and then he will begin with enthusiasm the business that will recompense him. Only such an one may truly be called a Master of Nature, for any other mere naturalist will only awaken the sense of Nature fortuitously and sympathetic-ally as being himself a manifestation of Nature.

THE STORY OF
HYACINTH AND ROSEBLOSSOM

Translated by Lillie Winter

Long ages ago there lived in the far west a guileless youth. He was very good, but at the same time peculiar beyond measure. He constantly grieved over nothing at all, always went about alone and silent, sat down by himself whenever the others played and were happy, and was always thinking about strange things. Woods and caves were his favorite haunts, and there he talked constantly with birds and animals, with rocks and trees--naturally not a word of sense, nothing but stuff silly enough to make one die a-laughing. Yet he continued to remain morose and grave in spite of the fact that the squirrel, the long-tailed monkey, the parrot, and the bullfinch took great pains to distract him and lead him into the right path. The goose would tell fairy-tales, and in the midst of them the brook would tinkle a ballad; a great heavy stone would caper about ludicrously; the rose stealing up affectionately behind him would creep through his locks, and the ivy stroke his careworn forehead. But his melancholy and his gravity were obstinate. His parents were greatly grieved; they did not know what to do. He was healthy and ate well. His parents had never hurt his feelings, nor until a few years since had any one been more cheerful and lively than he; always he had been at the head of every game, and was well liked by all the girls. He was very handsome indeed, looked like a picture, danced beautifully. Among the girls there was one sweet and very pretty child.

She looked as though she were of wax, with hair like silk spun of gold, lips as red as cherries, a figure like a little doll, eyes black as the raven. Such was her charm that whoever saw her might have pined away with love. At that time Roseblossom, that was her name, cherished a heart-felt affection for the handsome Hyacinth, that was his name, and he loved her with all his life. The other children did not know it. A little violet had been the first to tell them; the house-cats had noticed it, to be sure, for their parents' homes stood near each other. When, therefore, Hyacinth was standing at night at his window and Roseblossom at hers, and the pussies ran by on a mouse-hunt, they would see both standing, and would often laugh and titter so loudly that the children would hear them and grow angry. The violet had confided it to the strawberry, she told it to her friend, the gooseberry, and she never stopped taunting when Hyacinth passed; so that very soon the whole garden and the goods heard the news, and whenever Hyacinth went out they called on every side: "Little Roseblossom is my sweetheart!" Now Hyacinth was vexed, and again he could not help laughing from the bottom of his heart when the lizard would come sliding up, seat himself on a warm stone, wag his little tail, and sing

Little Roseblossom, good and kind,
Suddenly was stricken blind.
Her mother Hyacinth she thought
And to embrace him forthwith sought.
But when she felt the face was strange,
Just think, no terror made her change!
But on his cheek pressed she her kiss,
And she had noted naught amiss.

Alas, how soon did all this bliss pass away! There came along a man from foreign lands; he had traveled everywhere, had a long beard, deep-set eyes, terrible eyebrows, a strange cloak with many folds and queer figures woven in it. He seated himself in front of the

★ 49

house that belonged to Hyacinth's parents. Now Hyacinth was very curious and sat down beside him and fetched him bread and wine. Then the man parted his white beard and told stories until late at night and Hyacinth did not stir nor did he tire of listening. As far as one could learn afterward the man had related much about foreign lands, unknown regions, astonishingly wondrous things, staying there three days and creeping down into deep pits with Hyacinth. Roseblossom cursed the old sorcerer enough, for Hyacinth was all eagerness for his tales and cared for nothing, scarcely even eating a little food. Finally the man took his departure, not, however, without leaving Hyacinth a booklet that not a soul could read. The youth had even given him fruit, bread, and wine to take along and had accompanied him a long way. Then he came back melancholy and began an entirely new mode of life. Roseblossom grieved for him very pitifully, for from that time on he paid little attention to her and always kept to himself.

Now it came about that he returned home one day and was like one new-born. He fell on his parents' neck and wept. "I must depart for foreign lands," he said; "the strange old woman in the forest told me that I must get well again; she threw the book into the fire and urged me to come to you and ask for your blessing. Perhaps I shall be back soon, perhaps never more. Say good-bye to Roseblossom for me. I should have liked to speak to her, I do not know what is the matter, something drives me away; whenever I want to think of old times, mightier thoughts rush in immediately; my peace is gone, my courage and love with it, I must go in quest of them. I should like to tell you whither, but I do not know myself; thither where dwells the mother of all things, the veiled virgin. For her my heart burns. Farewell!"

He tore himself away and departed. His parents lamented and shed tears. Roseblossom kept in her chamber and wept bitterly. Hyacinth now hastened as fast as he could through valleys and wildernesses, across mountains and streams, toward the mysterious country. Everywhere he asked men and animals, rocks and trees, for the sacred goddess (Isis). Some laughed, some were silent, nowhere did he receive an answer. At first he passed through wild, uninhabited regions, mist and clouds obstructed his path, it was always storming; later he found unbounded deserts of glowing hot sand, and as he wandered his mood changed, time seemed to grow longer, and his inner unrest was calmed. He became more tranquil and the violent excitement within him was gradually transformed to a gentle but strong impulse, which took possession of his whole nature. It seemed as though many years lay behind him. Now, too, the region again became richer and more varied, the air warm and blue, the path more level; green bushes attracted him with their pleasant shade but he did not understand their language, nor did they seem to speak, and yet they filled his heart with verdant colors, with quiet and freshness. Mightier and mightier grew within him that sweet longing, broader and softer the leaves, noisier and happier the birds and animals, balmier the fruits, darker the heavens, warmer the air and more fiery his love; faster and faster passed the Time, as though it knew that it was approaching the goal.

One day he came upon a crystal spring and a bevy of flowers that were going down to a valley between black columns reaching to the sky. With familiar words they greeted him kindly. "My dear countrymen," he said, "pray, where am I to find the sacred abode of Isis? It must be somewhere in this vicinity, and you are probably better acquainted here than I." "We, too, are only passing through this region," the flowers answered; "a family of spirits is traveling and we are making ready the road and preparing lodgings for them; but we came through a region lately where we heard her name called. Just walk upward in the direction from which we are coming and you will be sure to learn more." The flowers and the spring smiled as they said this, offered him a drink of fresh water, and went on.

Hyacinth followed their advice, asked and asked, and finally reached that long-sought dwelling concealed behind palms and other choice plants. His heart beat with infinite longing and the most delicious yearning thrilled him in this abode of the eternal seasons. Amid heavenly fragrance he fell into slumber, since naught but dreams might lead him to the most sacred place. To the tune of charming melodies and in changing harmonies did his dream guide him mysteriously through endless apartments filled with curious things. Everything seemed so familiar to him and yet amid a splendor that he had never seen; then even the last tinge of earthliness vanished as though dissipated in the air, and he stood before the celestial virgin. He lifted the filmy, shimmering veil and Roseblossom fell into his arms. From afar a strain of music accompanied the mystery of the loving reunion, the outpourings of their longing, and excluded all that was alien from this delightful spot. After that Hyacinth lived many years with Roseblossom near his happy parents and comrades, and innumerable grandchildren thanked the mysterious old woman for her advice and her fire; for at that time people got as many children as they wanted.

Novalis

Novalis

Sophie von Kühn

TRANSCENDENT POETRY:
A NOTE ON NOVALIS

The world must be romanticized.

Novalis, *Pollen and Fragments* (56)

Poetry is what is truly and absolutely real, this is the kernel of my philosophy. The more poetic, the more true.

Novalis[1]

Novalis is the most mystical of the German Romantic poets. He is at once the most typical and the most unusual of the German Romantic poets – indeed, of all Romantic poets.[2] He is supremely idealistic, far more so than Johann Wolfgang von Goethe or Heinrich Heine. He died young, which makes him, like Percy Bysshe Shelley and John Keats, something of a hero (or martyr). He did not write as much as Shelley,

1 Novalis: *Works*(Minor), III, 11
2 See Richard Faber, 1970; Heinz Ritter: "Die geistlichen Lieder des Novalis. Ihre Datierung und Entstehung", *Jahrbuch der deutschen Schiller–Gesellschaft* IV, 1960, 308–42; Friedrich Hiebel: *Novalis*, Francke, Bern 1972; Curt Grutzmacher, 1964; Géza von Molnár, 1970; John Neubauer, 1972; Bruce Haywood, 1959.

but his work, like that of Keats or Arthur Rimbaud, promised much. For Michael Hamburger, Novalis' work is almost totally idealistic: 'Novalis's philosophy, then, is not mystical, but utopian. That is why his imaginative works are almost wholly lacking in conflict. They are a perpetual idyll'.[3] It's true, Novalis' work is supremely idealistic, and utopian. But it is also mystical, because it points towards the invisible, unseen, unknown, and aims to reach that ecstatic realm. He wrote:

> The sense of poetry has much in common with that for mysticism. It is the sense of the peculiar, personal, unknown, mysterious, for what is to be *revealed*, the necessary-accidental. It represents the unrepresentable. It sees the invisible, feels the unfeelable, etc... The sense for poetry has a close relationship with the sense for augury and the religious sense, with the sense for prophecy in general.[4]

Novalis was born Georg Philipp Friedrich von Hardenberg on May 2, 1772 in Oberwiederstedt. He studied law between 1790 and 1794 at Jena, Wittenberg and Leipzig. There he met many of the leading literary lights, such as Johann Wolfgang von Goethe, Johann Gottfried Herder, Jean Paul (Johann Paul Friedrich Richter), the Schlegels, Ludwig von Tieck and Friedrich Wilhelm Joseph Schelling. Later, in 1797, Novalis studied at the Mining Academy in Freiburg. He began publishing in 1798. His chief works include: *Faith and Love or the King and the Queen, Pollen, The Novices at Sais, Heinrich von Ofterdingen, Christendom or Europa* and *Hymns To the Night*.[5] He was engaged to Sophie von Kühn from 1794-97, and to Julie von Charpentier from 1798 to his death in 1801. He died on March 25, 1801 in Weißenfels, from tuberculosis.

Novalis was passionately in love with his beloved, Sophie, whom he had met in October, 1794, when she was twelve. They were engaged in

---

3 M. Hamburger: *Reason and Energy*, 97
4 Novalis: *Novalis Schriften*, 3, 686
5 The translator of this edition of *Hymns To the Night*, George MacDonald (1824-95), was influenced by Novalis. MacDonald's works included *Phantastes* (1858), *Lilith* (1895), *Bannerman's Boyhood* and the *Curdie* children's stories: *The Princess and the Goblin*(1872) and *The Princess and Curdie*(1882). Lewis Carroll and John Ruskin were among MacDonald's literary friends. The Scottish fantasist was a significant influence on J.R.R. Tolkien and C.S. Lewis, among others.

March, 1795 (Sophie was 13; Novalis was 22). Novalis was devastated when she died on March 19, 1797, two days after her fifteenth birthday. 'My main task should be', he wrote, 'to bring everything into a relationship to [Sophia's] idea.'[6]

After the death of Sophia von Kühn, Novalis wrote to Karl Wilhelm Friedrich Schlegel from Tennstedt, near Grüningen, where she was buried:

> You can imagine how I feel in this neighbourhood, the old witness of my and her glory. I still feel a secret enjoyment to be so close to her grave. It attracts me ever more closely, and this now occasionally constitutes my indescribable happiness. My autumn has come, and I feel so free, usually so vigorous – something can come of me after all. This much I solemnly assure you as become absolutely clear to me what a heavenly accident her death has been – the key to everything – a marvellously appropriate event. Only through it could various things be absolutely resolved and much immaturity overcome. A simple mighty force has come to reflection within me. My love has become a flame gradually consuming everything earthly.[7]

Sophie von Kühn was for Novalis something like Dante Alighieri's Beatrice Portinari or Francesco Petrarch's Laura de Noyes, or Maurice Scève's Délie; that is, a soul–image or *anima* figure, someone pure and holy. Further, Sophie the person fused for Novalis with 'Sophia' of Gnostic philosophy, the Goddess about whom C.G. Jung has written so eloquently.

> My favourite study [wrote Novalis in 1796] has the same name as my fiancée. Sophie is her name – philosophy is the soul of my life and the key to my inner-most self. Since that acquaintance, I also have become completely amalgamated with that study.[8]

Sophia is the Goddess of Wisdom; she is an incarnation for poets and mystics of the Black Goddess, a deity who presides over the unknown, the dark things, occultism and witchcraft. Novalis was very interested in the occult, in magic and hermeticism, in Neoplatonism, alchemy, theosophy, the *Qabbalah*, and other belief systems. Novalis was

---

6 Novalis: ib, 4, 37
7 Novalis, in, 4, 220
8 Novalis, letter to Friedrich Schlegel, 8 July 1796, in *Novalis Schriften*, op.cit., 4, 188

fascinated by the invisible realm, the things that are unseen but he knows are there, which is the realm of occultism. As he writes: 'We are bound nearer to the unseen than to the visible.'[9]

Apart from his small collection of lyrics, and his *Hymnen an die Nacht,* one of Novalis' major works was his (unfinished) *Blütenstaub (Pollen)* and *Glauben und Liebe (Faith and Love),* collections of philosophical fragments. These together form an æsthetics of religion, and a mysticism of poetry.

❦

Some notes on German Romanticism are worth making here: the world of German Romantic poetry holds many of the same tenets as that of British and French Romanticism. The term 'Romanticism' means for me here a lyrical, emotional, religious and self-conscious form of art which can be applied to many modern artists, as well as the Romantics themselves.[10]

One of the key elements of Romantic poetry, of German Romantic poetry especially, and of all poetry generally, is the concept of unity. For the poet, all things are connected together.

> In our mind [wrote Novalis], everything is connected in the most peculiar, pleasant, and lively manner. The strangest things come together by virtue of one space, one time, an odd similarity, an error, some accident. In this manner, curious unities and peculiar connections originate – one thing reminds us of everything, becomes the sign of many things. Reason and imagination are united through time and space in the most extraordinary manner, and we can say that each thought, each phenomenon of our mind is the most individual part of an altogether individual totality.[11]

What connects everything is the poet's sensibility, awareness,

---

9 Novalis: *Pollen*, 125.
10 On Romanticism, see Jürgen Habermas: *The Philosophical Discourse of Modernity*, tr. Frederick Lawrence, MIT Press, Cambridge Mass., 1987. On German Romanticism, see David Simpson *et al*, eds: *German Aesthetic and Literary Criticism*, Cambridge University Press, 3 vols, 1984–5; H.G. Schenk: *The Mind of the European Romantics*, Constable, 1966; M.H. Abrams: *Natural Supernaturalism: Tradition and Revolution in Romantic Literature*, Norton, New York, 1971; Marshall Brown, 1979; Philippe Lacoue–Labarthe & Jean-Luc Nancy, eds, 1988; Azade Seyhan: *Representation and its Discontents: The Critical Legacy of German Romanticism*, University of California Press, Berkeley, 1992.
11 Novalis, *Novalis Schriften*, 3, 650-1.

imagination, talents, feelings, call them what you will. Poetry is very much like Western magic in this respect. Magicians speak of the cardinal rule of hermeticism and magicke as being the hermetic tenet of the Emerald Table of Hermes Trismegistus: *as above, so below* This dictum applies to poetry as much to magic. Basically, the view is that all things are one even as they are separate/ different/ scattered everywhere. Sufi mystics speak of 'unity in multiplicity' and 'multiplicity in unity', the 'unity' for them being Allah. For poets and magicians, founded in the Western Neoplatonic, Renaissance, humanist, magical tradition, 'the One' is only occasionally identified with God.

For (the Romantic) poets, the *as above, so below* worldview means that inner and outer are identical, that what happens inside, psychologically, is mirrored and influences the outer, physical world. The two worlds interconnect and influence each other. As Novalis writes: 'What is outside me, is really within me, is mind – and vice versa'.[12] Further, the world is a continuum for the poet, so that colours are associated with particular planets, say, or angels, or flowers, or metals. This view of the oneness of all things occurs not only in Romantic poetry, but in most of poetry, from Sappho in the ancient world onwards. It is, partly, the basis for the 'pathetic fallacy', the ubiquitous poetic metaphor, where Sappho can say that erotic desire is like a wind shaking oak trees on a mountainside.

The Romantic philosophy of unity develops into Charles Baudelaire's 'theory of correspondences', which was later taken up by Arthur Rimbaud, Stéphane Mallarmé and Paul Valéry. Friedrich Schlegel, one of the major theorists of Romantic poetry, speaks of Romantic art as unifying poetry and philosophy, which is one of the hallmarks of Romantic poetry, German or otherwise. 'Romantic poetry is a progressive universal poetry', wrote Schlegel.[13] He argued for a new mythology of poetry, a universal mythopœia, which would connect all things together, a 'hieroglyphic expression of nature around us'.[14]

Folklore and fairy tales are another element: much of German

12 Novalis, *Novalis Schriften,* 3, 429
13 F. Schlegel: *Kritische Friedrich Schlegel Ausgabe,* Schöningh, Paderborn, 1958, II, 182
14 F. Schlegel, in ib., II, 318

Romanticism uses all kinds of folklore – the Grimms, for instance, with their very influential collection, *Children's and Household Tales*, and their collecting (and rewriting) of fairy tales. Ludwig von Tieck's works contain much fantastic material, and he uses fairy tales in his fictions, including Charles Perrault's *Puss in Boots* fairy tale in his *Der gestiefelte Kater*[15] A.W. Schlegel wrote: 'Myth, like language, generally, a necessary product of the human poetic power, an arche-poetry of humanity'.[16]

Novalis wrote of fairy tales: 'All fairy tales are dreams of that homelike world that is everywhere and nowhere.'[17] Figures such as Isolde and Tristan, Tannhäuser, of Arthurian legend, appear in German Romantic poetry. Romanticism also employs all manner of hermetic or occult thought, from Gnosticism (in Novalis's philosophy), Qabbalism, Rosicrucianism, alchemy, magic, astronomy, etc (in Franz Brentano's *Die Romanzen vom Rosenkrantz* alchemy in Johann Wolfgang von Goethe's *Faust*, etc).

The Hellenism of German Romanticism ties in with (and is inextricable from) the paganism of Romanticism. The German Romantics, like their British counterparts, exalted pagan beliefs, though theirs was a stylized, self-conscious form of paganism, which took up certain beliefs or rites and ignored others. Heinrich Heine wrote that the first Romantics

acted out of a pantheistic impulse of which they themselves were not aware. The feeling which they believed to be a nostalgia for the Catholic Mother Church was of deeper origin than they guessed, and their reverence and preference for the heritage of the Middle Ages, for the popular beliefs, diabolism, magical practices, and witchcraft of that era... all this was a suddenly reawakened but unrecognized leaning toward the pantheism of the ancient Germans.[18]

---

15 See Rolf Stamm: *Ludwig Tieck's späte Novellen*, Kohlhamer, Stuttgart, 1973; Raimund Belgardt: "Poetic Imagination and External Reality in Tieck", *Essays in German Literature Festschrift* ed. Michael S. Batts, University of British Columbia Press, 1968, 41-61; Rosemarie Helge: *Motive und Motivstrukturen bei Ludwig Tieck*, Kummerle, Göppingen, 1974
16 A.W. Schlegel: *Kritische Ausgabe der Verlesungen* ed. Ernst Behler & Frank Jolles, Schöningen, Paderborn, 1989-, I, 49
17 Novalis, *Novalis Schriften*, 2. 564
18 H. Heine: *Salon II*, 1852, 250-1

The paganism of Romanticism is a part of pantheism, as in the Classicism of painters such as Nicolas Poussin and Claude Lorrain, or nature worship. Heinrich Heine called pantheism 'the secret religion of Germany'.[19]

The Romantics, including Novalis, exalted nature (German Romanticism had its 'Naturphilosophie', a non-scientific notion stemming partly from the work of Friedrich Wilhelm Joseph Schelling and Georg Wilhelm Friedrich Hegel). But, again, nature is mediated through the highly self-conscious and heavily stylized mechanisms of poetry. Images of nature abound in most forms of Romantic poetry. Nature is the backdrop to their poetic out-pourings, but it is always nature seen from the vantage point of culture.[20]

German Romantic poetry, like all Romantic poetry (like all poetry, one might say), has idealistic and utopian elements. German Romantic poetry, in particular, is marked by a vivacious, sometimes over-developed idealism (and utopianism), which comes as much from the philosopher Plato as from Immanuel Kant. 'Transcendental idealism' is a term often applied to German Romantic poetics. 'I call transcendental all knowledge which is not so much occupied with objects as with the mode of our cognition of objects', remarked Kant in the *Critique of Pure Reason*,[21] underlining the subjectivity (as with René Descartes) that is at the centre of post-Renaissance philosophy. There is a philosophy, Johann Gottlieb Fichte argued, that is beyond being and beyond consciousness, a philosophy that aims for 'the absolute unity between their separateness.'[22]

❧

Novalis, like the other (German) Romantics, believed in the magical/ religious unity of the world. For him, all things were united, in one way or another. Novalis was one of the first artists to bring together many seemingly diverse practices and philosophies. Leonardo da Vinci had

19 H. Heine: *Works*, 3, 571
20 Novalis has a fascinating view of nature as the mother, a refuge: 'the reason why people are so attached to Nature is probably that, being spoilt children, they are afraid of the father and take refuge with the mother'.
21 Immanuel Kant: *Werke*, de Gruyter, Berlin, 1968, III, 43
22 J. Fichte, letter, 23 June 1804, quoted in E. Behler, 19

drawn together botany, biology, anatomy, natural science, engineering, mathematics and other strands of thought in his Renaissance art, and Novalis did the same. The metaphysical synthesis was called *Totalwissenschaft*, a total knowledge.

Novalis learnt much from Friedrich Schlegel, during his time at Jena, one of the centres of German Romanticism. Schlegel wrote at length of the unifying spirit of art, where poetry and philosophy merge: the aim of Romantic poetry, Schlegel asserted, was not only 'to unite all the separate species of poetry and put poetry in touch with philosophy and rhetoric', but also to

> use poetry and prose, inspiration and criticism, the poetry of art and the poetry of nature; and make poetry lively and sociable, and life and society poetic; poeticize wit and fill and saturate the forms of art with every kind of good, solid matters for instruction, and animate them with the pulsation of humour.[23]

Novalis' philosophy may be called 'transcendent philosophy', as his poetry might be called 'transcendent poetry'. He called it 'magisch', 'Magie', his 'magic idealism'.[24] It is a mixture of poetry and philosophy, a poetry of philosophy and a philosophy of poetry.[25] 'Transcendental poetry is an admixture of poetry and philosophy,'[26] he writes. And again: 'Poetry is the champion of philosophy... Philosophy is the theory of poetry.' (ib., 56) Poetry becomes philosophy, and philosophy becomes poetry. Or as he put it: 'Die Welt wird Traum, der Traum wird Welt' ('World becomes dream, dream becomes world'). Friedrich Schlegel wrote in the *Athenæum* (fragment 451): 'Universality can attain harmony only through the conjunction of poetry and philosophy'.[27]

Kept by Novalis as a collection of fragments, *Pollen* has affinities with the maxims of Friedrich Nietzsche, the thoughts in Blaise Pascal's

---

23 F. Schlegel, *Gespräch über die Poesie, Kritische Friedrich Schlegel Ausgabe* Schöningh, Paderborn, 1958, 182
24 Novalis: *Works* (Minor), Paris, 1837, III
25 See Manfred Frank: "Die Philosophie des sogenannten "magischen Idealismus"", *Euph*, LXIII, 1969, 88–116; Karl Heinz Volkmann–Schluck, 1967, 45–53; Theodor Haering, 1954; G. Hughes, 66; Manfred Dick, 1967, 223–77; Hugo Kuhn: *Text und Theorie*, Metzler, Stuttgart 1967
26 Novalis: *Pollen and Fragments*, 57
27 F. Schlegel, *Lucinde and the Fragments*, tr. Peter Firchow, University of Minnesota Press, Minneapolis 1971, 240

Pensées, with Jacob Boehme's writings and other mystical collections. It is worth quoting from some of these fragments, which show Novalis at his most idealistic and pithy. His statements summarize the (German) Romantic position on poetry, and the basics of all poetics. First of all, he muses on interiority:

> Toward the Interior goes the arcane way. In us, or nowhere, is the Eternal with its worlds, the past and future... The seat of the world is there, where the inner world and the outer world touch... The inner world is almost more mine than the outer. It is so heartfelt, so private – man is given fullness in that life – it is so native.[28]

Here Novalis heads straight for one of the prime realms of mysticism: the inner world, the life of the spirit, the imagination, the soul. His distinction, and then fusion, of inner and outer is the beginnings of modern psychology. It is also one of the key aspects of poetry. For the poet, the inner, psychic or spiritual world is as real and as important, and nourishing, as the outer, public world. The two in fact are part of a continuum, both flowing into each other, like the *yin–yang* dualism of Chinese mysticism. The one informs the other in art. They are not separated, that is the key point. They form a unity. As Novalis wrote in his poem 'Know Yourself' (the title comes from the basic tenet of Greek hermeticism): 'There is only one'.[29]

In magic and hermeticism, the fundamental tenet is 'as above, so below', which, in the modern era, becomes the psychological 'as outside, so inside'. Poets have long known about this inside–outside pairing. In William Shakespeare's plays, the external setting of a scene – the opening of *Macbeth,* for instance – indicates the characters' inner feelings. Further, in Shakespeare's Elizabethan theatre, there were few props, and little scenery on stage, so the words became full of images, painting pictures in the audience's mind. Hence, in a different way, inner and outer became fused.

For Novalis, rightly, the seat of the soul is precisely that poetic space where 'the inner world and the outer world touch' (150). It was Rainer Maria Rilke who fully developed this inner–outer unity in his

28 Novalis: *Pollen and Fragments*, 50-53
29 Novalis: *Pollen*, 137

lyrics. Rilke is, as we have said, the poet most like Novalis in German poetry. Rilke had his notion of the Angel (in the *Duino Elegies*). The Rilkean Angel is essentially a shaman, and Novalis also speaks at length in his collections of fragments of the poet as shaman. He does not use the term 'shaman', but his 'sorcerer' or 'genius' or 'prophet' is basically the archaic shaman, the angelic traveller to other worlds, the vatic mouthpiece of his/ her cult, the dancing, drumming, musical figure, like Dionysius or Orpheus, who knows how to fly, who can climb the World Tree, who can penetrate the invisible.[30] Novalis writes:

> The sorcerer is a poet. The prophet is to the sorcerer as the man of taste is to the poet... The genuine poet is all–knowing... (50–1)

As Weston La Barre notes in *The Ghost Dance*, there is not much difference between the artist, the genius, the criminal, the psychotic and the mad person. Novalis notes:

> Madness and magic have many similarities. A magician is an artist of madnesses. (79)

Similarly, William Shakespeare wrote in *A Midsummer Night's Dream*: 'The lunatic, the lover and the poet,/ Are of imagination all compact.' (V.i.7) In Shakespeare's art, there are deep connections between lovers, lunatics, poets – and fools. They are all caught up with some kind of 'madness', some kind of 'abnormal', 'extraordinary' subjectivity. Their goals may be different, but they are all connected psychologically. Similarly, for Novalis, as for so many poets, love can be seen as a madness, and there is a narrow dividing line between the religious maniac and the fool. There is the 'holy fool' figure in Russian history, the 'trickster god' in ancient mythology, and King Lear's clown, the court jester who is allowed to transgress the boundaries that others are not allowed to cross.

Novalis as a poet sees the unity of all things, so he writes: 'All barriers are only there for the traversing' (87). This is the Romantic

---

30 See Mircea Eliade, *Myths, Dreams and Mysteries*, Harper & Row, New York, 1975; *Shamanism: Archaic Techniques of Ecstasy* Princeton University Press, New Jersey, 1972; Weston La Barre: *The Ghost Dance*, Allen & Unwin 1972

poet talking here: this is a very Romantic notion, it seems, this perception that barriers are there to be transgressed. This is the poet as social rebel speaking, knowing that art must go to extremes. Thus, madness, poetry, idiocy, genius and love form a continuum which is life itself.

In Novalis's *œuvre*, love and mysticism, the secular and the sacred, art and religion, fuse. Thus, in Novalis' 'magic idealism', we hear of the mysticism of love, or the religious nature of art. In this he is no different from other Romantics, such as William Wordsworth or Victor Hugo. For Novalis, life itself is sacred. 'Our whole life is a divine service', he writes (124). In this Novalis is in accord with writers such as D.H. Lawrence, who regarded life itself as holy, or the artist and sculptor Eric Gill, or the cult of the Australian aborigines.

The religion of the aborigines is the 'eternal dreamtime', the mythic, timeless state. For them, life was sacred, and life was sacralized by rituals that include singing. The Australian Bushmen speak of 'singing the world into life'. Rainer Maria Rilke wrote in his *Sonnets For Orpheus*: 'song is existence.' The figure of Orpheus, the mythological poet–as–shaman, features prominently, though he is sometimes hidden, in the works of poets such as Novalis (in his story *Heinrich von Ofterdingen*), Rilke and Arthur Rimbaud. Orpheus' song is his art, and his *raison d'être*. Novalis also wrote of music, and its relation to poetry and religion. The notion of the 'music of the spheres', the celestial harmonies that drive the cosmos, is central to Western religion. For Dante Alighieri, God was at the centre of the concentric circles or wheels of the universe. He was at the heart of the *Rosa Mystica*. For Novalis, the 'One' of Neoplatonism now has many names. In Hinduism it is Brahma; in Taoism it is the Tao; in Zen Buddhism it is Pure Reality; in Tibetan mysticism it is the Clear Light of the Void; and in Islam it is Allah.

Simply being alive, as Mircea Eliade notes, was a sacred act:

> In the most archaic phases of culture, *to live as a human being* was in itself *a religious act*, since eating, sexual activity, and labour all had a sacramental value. Experience of the sacred is inherent in man's mode of being in the

world.[31]

D.H. Lawrence wrote extensively of 'being alive', about real 'livingness'. In *Etruscan Places* he defined it in a way of which Novalis would surely approve:

> To the Etruscan all was alive...They [the Etruscans] felt the symbols and danced the sacred dances. For they were always in touch, physically, with the mysteries.[32]

Novalis speaks often of 'mysteries' too. For the occult, hermetic, Neoplatonic, religious artist, there must always be some 'mystery' behind everything. No matter how far you go, there must always be something mysterious behind it. It was true for the participants in the ancient Eleusian Mysteries, and it is the same for Romantic poets. The world is not a machine, nor is it limited. It must be infinite, for, behind everything, there is yet more mystery. There are no limits, yet it is the poet's task to find the limits, and to explore the boundaries.

Novalis looked back to early Christianity, to Neoplatonism and to Greek religion. Like most Romantics, Novalis was very nostalgic. But he might have looked back also to many Hindu sects, to Tantric cults, to Sufi mystics and poets, to Australian aborigines, to the shamans of Siberia and North America, to the Chinese Taoists (Chuang–tzu, Lao–tzu), or to the Confucians (Confucius, Mencius), or to the Zen Buddhist masters (Hui–Neng, Dogen, Jakuin), or to the Ancient Greeks of Epicurus, Heraclitus or Empodecles' day.

What is the purpose of Novalis' cult of 'transcendent poetry'? More life, basically. This was Rainer Maria Rilke's great goal, his Holy Grail: life and more life, more and more of life. That is our goal, Rilke claimed. Poetry is a way of enabling us to be more alive, say Novalis and Rilke:

> Poetry is the great art of constructing transcendental health... Poetry is generation. All compositions must be living individuals. (*Pollen*, 50)

31 Mircea Eliade, *Ordeal by Labyrinth*, University of Chicago Press 1984, 154
32 D.H. Lawrence: *Mornings in Mexico and Etruscan Places*, Penguin 1960, 147–9

Rainer Maria Rilke says similar things about poetry. In a letter to his Polish translator, Witold von Hulewicz, of November 13, 1925, Rilke explained his notion of the angel: a being that shows us how to be painfully but blissfully alive, living in the transcendent realm of 'the Open', as Rilke called that special poetic place. We must be

> Transformed? Yes, for our task is to stamp this provisional, perishing earth into ourselves so deeply, so painfully and passionately, that its being may rise again, "invisibly", in us.[33]

All you have to do in life is to be. Be what, exactly? Just *be*, says Rainer Maria Rilke: 'all we basically have to do is to *be*, but simply, earnestly, the way the earth simply is', he wrote in *Letters on Cézanne*[34] To simply *be* is really difficult, as Novalis and Rilke admit. Yet it is the goal. To realize, as the Hindu mystics put it, that Thou Art That (*tat tvam asi*). As Novalis commented:

> Art of becoming all–powerful. Art of realizing our intentions totally. (118)

Total fulfilment – it's a tall order, perhaps, but only this ontological totality will do for Novalis. He is supremely idealistic while at the same being totally honest, and totally simple, and totally ordinary. He is optimistic, it seems, when he writes:

> All is seed. (73)

Yet he is also being quite realistic, knowing, as an artist does, that *anything* can be used in art. A transcendent, total art can include *everything.* Nothing is exempt from art, not even nothingness itself. Indeed, nothingness is a large element of some art (Samuel Beckett's compressed texts, for instance, or Ad Reinhardt's black–on–black paintings), as it is a key component in Buddhism and Taoism.

Novalis' idealistic philosophy is all–inclusive. 'All is seed', he writes.

---

33 Rilke: *Duino Elegies,* tr. J.B. Leishman & Stephen Spender, Hogarth Press, 1957, 157
34 Rilke: *Letters on Cézanne* ed. Clara Rilke, Cape, 1988

All. Or, again, in a different fashion:

All must become nourishment. (65)

Or, again, in a different way, he says:

All can become experiment – all can become an organ. (88)

Meister Eckhart, the German mediæval mystic whose mystical philosophy is in tune with Rainer Maria Rilke's and Novalis' philosophies, wrote:

> The seed of God is in us... The seed of a pear tree grows into a pear tree, a hazel seed into a hazel tree, a seed of God into God.[35]

Much of alchemy, hermeticism, witchcraft, Qabbalism and Neoplatonism is concerned with healing, nourishment and rebirth. It was one of Novalis' chief concerns. The philosophical fragments state the basic view of nourishment in a variety of ways. The fragments are deeply poetic. Although they are written in prose, they are clearly poetry. One of Novalis' most powerful sentences is:

Everything can become magical work. (73)

This statement is itself magical. For Novalis, art is for the enrichment of life. Whatever art may do, Novalis says, it must enrich us. 'To enliven all is the aim of life', he asserts (64).

❧

Love features prominently in Novalis' philosophy of poetry and poetry of philosophy. Love – and sex. For, under Novalis' sophisticated sophisms, there is sex. An eroticism which is that fundamental *jouissance* of the text in Romanticism is found in Novalis's work. For Novalis, love and philosophy are aspects of the same mystery. 'It is with love as with philosophy', he writes (*Pollen*, 57). He evokes the *eroticism* of philosophy, something which Plato may have understood

---

35 Quoted in James M. Clark & John V. Skinner: *Meister Eckhart,* London 1953, 151

subconsciously, but which Novalis brings into the foreground:

> In the essential sense, philosophizing is – a caress – a testimony to the inner love of reflection, the absolute delight of wisdom. (53)

For Novalis, the highest form of love is spiritual, of course. In this he is in harmony with those other great poets of love, such as Dante Alighieri, Francesco Petrarch, Guido Guinicelli, Guido Cavalcanti and Bernard de Ventadour. For the mediæval troubadours and *stilnovisti*, human love was transcended in stature and significance by spiritual love. In personal terms, this meant that the human, flesh–and–blood beloved, Petrarch's Laura, Dante's Beatrice, Novalis' Sophie, was surpassed, spiritually, and even transcended physically in some cases, by the figure of the Virgin Mary. Novalis too, like Dante and Petrarch, raised the Mother of God above his Sophie as a beloved.

> By absolute will power, love can be gradually transmuted into religion.[36]

This is a familiar pose with (usually male) poets, this worldly renunciation in favour of religious love. 'What I feel for Sophie', Novalis wrote, 'is religion, not love' (ib., 295).

Friedrich Nietzsche had a theory that the more tragic tragedy becomes, the more sensual it becomes. In other words, tragedy has a sensual dimension which increases as the sense of tragedy increases. William Shakespeare's tragedies are his most erotic works. Think of the erotic entanglements of love and death in *Macbeth*, or *King Lear*. Novalis too spoke of the erotic quality of intensity and absolutism. Power is an aphrodisiac, it is said: the powerful people are those who can go to extremes. Tragic characters go to extremes – Macbeth, Beatrice, Othello – they push against their ontological boundaries. They practice a kind of absolutism or extremism that seems particularly Romantic. Novalis notes the sensuality of power and extremism in his fragments, as when he claims:

> All absolute sensation is religious. (197)

---

36 Novalis, *Works* (Minor) II, 299

Tragic power and political power is sexual and seductive, and so is magical power. Novalis writes:

Magic is like art – to wilfully use the sensual realm. (119)

Magicians throughout history have been erotic figures: Aleister Crowley, Georg Gurdjieff, Merlin, Paracelsus. The eroticism of magic is obvious: witchcraft, for instance, was and is regarded very much in sexual terms. Witchcraft was a heresy, certainly, that disturbed the Church for religious reasons, but many of the accusations brought against witchcraft were of a sexual nature.

More 'ordinary' – that is, bourgeois, heterosexual, traditional – are the views of Novalis on love such as this:

Every beloved object is the focus of a paradise... One touches heaven, when one touches a human body. (30, 59)

This neatly summarizes the links between love and religion that have been described throughout history, from the Biblical *Song of Songs* onwards. Novalis says that you touch heaven when you touch a body. This is what the troubadours said, that making love was heavenly, that to enter a woman was to enter heaven. William Shakespeare said it, John Donne said it, John Keats said it, and Robert Graves said it in the British poetic tradition; Sappho and C.P. Cavafy said it in the Greek tradition; Ovid, Dante Alighieri and Giuseppe Ungaretti said it in the Italian tradition; Novalis, Joseph Freiherr von Eichendorff, Ludwig von Tieck and Rainer Maria Rilke said it in the German tradition; Alexander Pushkin, Fyodor Tyutchev, Arseny Tarkovsky and Anna Akhmatova said it in the Russian tradition.

Not all of Novalis' eroticism was cerebral, philosophic and 'idealistic'. He produced obvious eroticism at times, the sensual love of a beloved which centres on the body:

Wonderful powers of the bodily appearance – the beautiful lineaments – the form – the voice – the complexion – the musculature and elasticity – the eyes, the senses of touch, of feeling – the outer nature – the angles – the closed–off spaces – the darkness – the veil. Through the selection of clothing the body becomes yet more mystical. (116)

In Novalis' *Hymns To the Night*, the night itself is a vast, erotic, maternal, deep, dazzling space, the place of Henry Vaughan's 'deep, but dazzling darkness', the darkness of occultism and præternaturalism, the night that is the Goddess, the Mother Night of mythology, the Gnostic Night which is embodied in the Goddess Sophia, Wisdom, the night of shamanic flights. Rainer Maria Rilke in his *Duino Elegies*, wrote lyrically of this erotic night that whirls about humans and is full of angels:

> But, oh, the nights – those nights when the infinite wind
> eats at our faces! Who is immune to the night, to Night,
> ever–subtle, deceiving? Hardest of all, to the lonely,
> Night, is she gentler to lovers?[37]

Rainer Maria Rilke's poetic night is a bliss space which is clearly the external metaphor or image of the poet's inner space. It is a space of the invisible, where the Rilkean 'Open' can flourish. Novalis' night is similarly mythical:

> Downward I turn
> Toward the holy unspeakable
> Mysterious Night
> …The great wings of the spirit lift you aloft
> And fill us with joy
> Dark and unspeakable,
> Secret, as you yourself are,
> Joy that foreshadows
> A heaven to us.
> …Heavenly as flashing stars
> In each vastness
> Appear the infinite eyes
> Which the Night opens in us.[38]

Novalis, in his opening section of the *Hymns To the Night*, begins with that universal journey of heroes: into the underworld. It is a primary myth, this descent. In mythology it is often to Hell: Dante,

37 R. Rilke: *Duino Elegies*, tr. Stephen Cohn, Carcanet Press 1989, 21
38 Novalis: *Pollen*, 138–140

Orpheus, Jesus, and Isis: they descend into the underworld. Of course, by Novalis' epoch, this nocturnal realm was identified with the inner spaces. Novalis knew that the descent into an external, mythic space was the expression of an inner, psychic descent.

When he has made the shamanic journey into the unknown, invisible, dark realm, he finds... what? His beloved, his Muse, the Queen of the Night: veritably, the Black Goddess:

Praise the Queen of the World
The highest messenger
Of the holy world,
The one who nurtures
Holy love.
You come, Beloved –,
The Night is here –
My soul is enchanted –
The earthly day is past
And you are mine again.
I gaze into your deep dark eyes
And see nothing but love and ecstasy.
We sink upon the altar of Night
Upon the soft bed –
The veil drops
And kindled by your heated touch
The flame of the sweet offering
Glows. (140-1)

Novalis here describes the basic story or myth of Western culture: the descent and return, the journey to fundamental ontologies, the resacralization of life, symbolized by a spiritual union expressed in erotic terms. At the heart of the *Hymnen an die Nacht* is this erotic–spiritual union, an ecstatic fusion of dualities. It is also a poetic expression of lust, of masculinist desire. For, simply, the poet goes into the Night and he makes loves to it.

In Novalis' 1800 poem, despite the Christian and theological aspects of the work, the feminine, magical dimension is continually exalted. For Novalis, the Night is a womb out of which the Son of Light, Jesus, is born; but also, our era, the Christian epoch, is born from Mother Night. Novalis uses the typical mechanisms of shamanism – the night flight or spiritual journey – as a mythic descent and return. In section three of

Hymns to the Night, his soul soars over the world, in the typical fashion of archaic shamanism, which is the basis of all religion:

> You night raptures,
> Heavenly slumbers came over me
> The scene itself gently rose higher – my unbound, newborn
> Soul soared over the scene. The hill became a dust cloud
> and through the cloud I saw the clear features of my Beloved –
> In her eyes rested Eternity... (143)

Although he sees the mythic Night as Christian, a gathering darkness after the Light or Day of Greece, Novalis continually emphasizes the feminine, maternal aspects of this mythical Night. Novalis' Night, like Rainer Maria Rilke's, is a supremely female space: 'She bears *you* – motherly', he writes (143);

> The dark ocean's
> Blue depths
> Were a Goddess' womb.

There is much idealism in this view of a feminized soul-space, a mythic 'dreamtime' over which the Goddess presides. The upsurge of hope in the *Hymns To the Night* is very powerful:

> And into heaven's
> Infinite distance
> Filled with the lustrous world
> Into the heart of the highest spaces,
> The soul of the world withdrew
> With her powers
> To wait for the dawn
> Of new days
> And the higher destiny of the world. (150-1)

By the end of the poem, the transition is made, from the dark, maternal, feminine realm of Night to the bright, rational, masculine realm of Day or Light. 'We sink into the Father's heart', writes the poet, in the last line (159). But it is an ambiguous ending, for the new form of the feminine, the Virgin Mary, is not the erotic Black Goddess of ancient times.

Novalis describes the basic emotional displacement of the psychoanalysis of childhood: the movement of the child away from the mother towards the father; from intuition to ratiocination; from emotion to reason; from dependency to independence, from femininity to masculinity; from immaturity to maturity; from the semiotic realm to the symbolic realm (the Law of the Father).

Novalis simply trades in the usual poetic fare: the associations of darkness with the feminine, light with the masculine, and so on. He employs the age-old dichotomies of Western culture, where, after a night of ecstasy, the Night is renounced in favour of the Day. It is familiar rhetoric. Novalis, though, raises it to new heights because of his energy and idealism. *Hymns To the Night* is an exuberant poetic sequence, shot through and powered by flashes of inspiration and enthusiasm. It is a poem that exists all on its own. There is nothing else quite like it – not in German Romanticism, nor in poetry throughout history. It combines elements of the theological exegesis, the courtly *canso*, the philosophical tract, utopian and idealistic mysticism, and a fervent lyrical poetry.

Hymnen an die Nacht is a poem that embellishes the norms of Western culture – heterosexuality, theology, Christianity, and philosophy without much developing them or questioning them. It is an uncritical poem, which re-states what is already known – and felt – about Western culture. Ambiguity and doubt are not high in the poetic mix: *Hymnen an die Nacht* is a mystical poem, and about the certainty of the mystical experience. After their ecstasy, mystics feel utterly sure of their faith, their God, their duty, their life. They trust their mystical ecstasy, as one must trust one's own experiences in life. Romanticism, as we have seen, is founded on subjectivity. The Romantic poets, whether of France, Germany, Britain, America or Italy, unfailingly trust their own experiences. Indeed, artists must. Novalis' *Hymns To the Night* is constructed out of the basic, unshakeable faith in the poetic self.

❦

Novalis continues to be read, as do Heinrich Heine, Johann Wolfgang von Goethe, both Schlegels, Friedrich Schiller and Friedrich Hölderlin. There is a richness in poets such as Goethe and Novalis that endures. Glyn Hughes writes of Novalis:

❦ 77

The sustaining interest in the reading of Novalis's works is the sense of contact with a mind of visionary intensity and total commitment. The poetic achievement is in the momentary glimpses of ideal reality: what, in other contexts, we should call epiphanies. (61)

Novalis' *Hymns To the Night* articulates the rebirth at the heart of Romanticism, that self–invention which always goes to the heart of life by way of speaking of fundamental experiences – of love, death, birth and rebirth. From the womb of the Virgin Mother the shining self is reborn. Novalis' poetics, like those of Johann Wolfgang von Goethe, Friedrich Hölderlin, Heinrich Heine or Friedrich Schlegel, are those of a spiritual rebirth, a resacralization of life, a renaissance of life, in short. This is the goal of not just the Romantic poets, but of most poets throughout history.

Bibliography

BY NOVALIS

Recommended books are marked with an asterisk.

*Novalis Schriften. Die Werke Friedrichs von Hardenberg*ed. Richard Samuel,
   Hans-Joachim Mähl & Gerhard Schulz, Kohlhammer, Stuttgart, 1960-88 *
Pollen and Fragments: Selected Poetry and Prose, tr. Arthur Versluis, Phanes
   Press, Grand Rapids, 1989 *
Hymns to the Night and Other Selected Writings, tr. Charles E. Passage, Bobbs-
   Merrill Company, Indianapolis, 1960
Hymns to the Night, Treacle Press, New York, NY, 1978 *
Novalis: Fichte Studies, ed. J. Kneller, Cambridge University Press, Cambridge,
   2003
Notes For a Romantic Encyclopedia, tr. D. Wood, State University of New York
   Press, New York, 2007

ON NOVALIS

Henri Clemens Birven. *Novalis, Magus der Romantik*, Schwab, Büdingen, 1959
B. Donehower, ed. *The Birth of Novalis*, State University of New York Press, New
   York, 2007
Sara Frierichsmeyer. *The Androgyne In Early German Romanticism: Friedrich
   Schlegel, Novalis and the Metaphysics of Love* Bern, New York, 1983
Curt Grutzmacher. *Novalis und Philippe Otto Runge*, Eidos, Munich 1964
Bruce Haywood. *The Veil of Imagery: A Study of the Poetic Works of Friedrich
   von Hardenburg*, Harvard University Press, Cambridge, Mass., 1959
Frederick Heibel. *Novalis: German Poet, European Thinker, Christian Mystic*
   AMS, New York, 1969

L. Johns. *The Art of Recollection In Jena Romanticism* Niemeyer, Tübingen, 2002

Alice Kuzniar. *Delayed Endings: Nonclosure In Novalis and Hölderlin* ,University of Georgia Press, Athens, 1987

Géza von Molnar. *Novalis's Fichte Studies* Mouton, The Hague 1970

—. *Romantic Vision, Ethical Context: Novalis and Artistic Autonomy* University of Minnesota Press, Minneapolis 1987

Bruno Müller. *Novalis – der dichter als Mittler* Lang, Bern, 1984

John Neubauer. *Bifocal Vision: Novalis's Philosophy of Nature and Disease* , Chapel Hill 1972

—. *Novalis*, 1980

I. Nikolova. *Complementary Modes of Representation In Keats, Novalis and Shelley*, Peter Lang, New York, 2001

Nicholas Saul. *History and Poetry In Novalis and In the Tradition of the German Enlightenment*, Institute of Germanic Studies, 1984

OTHERS

Gwendolyn Bays. *The Orphic Vision: Seer Poets from Novalis to Rimbaud* University of Nebraska Press, Lincoln, 1964 *

Ernst Behler. *German Romantic Literary Theory,* Cambridge University Press, 1993 *

Ernst Benz. *The Mystical Sources of German Romantic Philosophy* tr. B. Reynolds & E. Paul, Pickwick, Allison Park, 1983

G. Birrell. *The Boundless Presence: Space and Time In the Literary Fairy Tales of Novalis and Tieck*, 1979

Richard Brinkmann, ed. *Romantik in Deutschland*, Metzler, Stuttgart, 1978

Manfred Brown. *The Shape of German Romanticism* Cornell University Press, Ithaca, 1979

K. Calhoun. *Fatherland: Novalis, Freud and the Discipline of Romance* 1992

Manfred Dick. *Die Entwicklung des Gedankens der Poesie in den Fragmenten des Novalis*, Bouvier, Bonn, 1967, 223-77

Hans Eichner. *Friedrich Schlegel*, Twayne, New York, 1970

R.W. Ewton. *The Literary Theory of A.W. Schlegel* Mouthon, The Hague, 1971

Richard Faber. *Novalis: die Phantasie an die Macht*, Metzler, Stuttgart 1970

Walter Feilchenfeld. *Der Einfluss Jacob Böhmes auf Novalis* Eberia, Berlin, 1922

Theodor Haering. *Novalis als Philosoph*, Kohlhammer, Stuttgart, 1954

Michael Hamburger. *Reason and Energy: Studies In German Literature* Weidenfeld & Nicolson, 1970 *

Heinrich Heine. *The Complete Poems of Heinrich Heine* tr. Hal Draper, Suhrkamp/ Insel, Boston, 1982

—. *The North Sea*, tr. Vernon Watkins, Faber, 1955

Friedrich Hölderlin. *Poems and Fragments*, tr. Michael Hamburger, Routledge & Kegan Paul, 1966

Glyn Tegai Hughes. *Romantic German Literature*, Edward Arnold, 1979 *

Philippe Lacoue-Labarthe & Jean-Luc Nancy, eds. *The Literary Absolute: The*

Theory of Literature In German Romanticism ,State University of New York
Press, Albany, 1988

D. Mahoney. *The Critical Fortunes of a Romantic Novel,*1994

J. Neubauer. *Novalis,* 1980

W. O'Brien. *Novalis,* 1995

Ritchie Robertson. *Heine,* Peter Halban, 1988

Helmut Schanze. *Romantik und Aufklärung, Unterschungen zu Friedrich Schlegel
und Novalis,* Carl, Nürnberg, 1966

—. ed. *Friedrich Schlegel und die Kunstheorie Seiner Zeit*Wissenschaftliche
Buchgesellschaft, Darmstadt, 1985

Elizabeth Sewell. *The Orphic Voice: Poetry and Natural History* ,Routledge,
1961*

Karl Heinz Volkmann-Schluck. "Novalis' magischer Idealismus", *Die deutsche
Romantik,* ed. Hans Steffen, 1967, 45-53

WEBSITES

Aquarium	novalis.autorenverzeichnis.de
Novalis Gesellschaft	novalis-gesellschaft.de
International Novalis Society	ula.org/s/or/en

Beauties, Beasts, and Enchantment

CLASSIC FRENCH FAIRY TALES

Translated and with an Introduction
by Jack Zipes

A collection of 36 classic French fairy tales translated by renowned writer Jack Zipes.
Cinderella, Beauty and the Beast, Sleeping Beauty and *Little Red Riding Hood* are among the
classic fairy tales in this amazing book.
Includes illustrations from fairy tale collections.
Jack Zipes has written and published widely on fairy tales.

'Terrific... a succulent array of 17th and 18th century 'salon' fairy tales'
- *The New York Times Book Review*

'These tales are adventurous, thrilling in a way fairy tales are meant to be... The translation
from the French is modern, happily free of archaic and hyperbolic language... a fine and
sophisticated collection' - *New York Tribune*

'Enjoyable to read... a unique collection of French regional folklore' - *Library Journal*

'Charming stories accompanied by attractive pen-and-ink drawings' - *Chattanooga Times*

Introduction and illustrations   612pp.   ISBN 9781861712510 Pbk   ISBN 9781861713193 Hbk

Arseny Tarkovsky

Selected Poems

Arseny Tarkovsky is the neglected Russian poet, father of the acclaimed film director Andrei Tarkovsky. This new book gathers together many of Tarkovsky's most lyrical and heartfelt poems, in Virginia Rounding's new, clear translations. Many of Tarkovsky's poems appeared in his son's films, such as *Mirror*, *Stalker*, *Nostalghia* and *The Sacrifice*. There is an introduction by Rounding, and a bibliography of both Arseny and Andrei Tarkovsky.

Illustrated. Bibliography and notes.
ISBN 9781816171711144 Pbk   ISBN 9781861712660 Hbk

CRESCENT MOON PUBLISHING

web: www.crmoon.com e-mail: cresmopub@yahoo.co.uk

ARTS, PAINTING, SCULPTURE

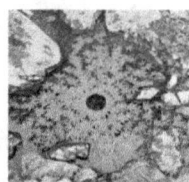

The Art of Andy Goldsworthy
Andy Goldsworthy: Touching Nature
Andy Goldsworthy in Close-Up
Andy Goldsworthy: Pocket Guide
Andy Goldsworthy In America
Land Art: A Complete Guide
The Art of Richard Long
Richard Long: Pocket Guide
Land Art In the UK
Land Art in Close-Up
Land Art In the U.S.A.
Land Art: Pocket Guide
Installation Art in Close-Up
Minimal Art and Artists In the 1960s and After
Colourfield Painting
Land Art DVD, TV documentary

Andy Goldsworthy DVD, TV documentary
The Erotic Object: Sexuality in Sculpture From Prehistory to the Present Day
Sex in Art: Pornography and Pleasure in Painting and Sculpture
Postwar Art
Sacred Gardens: The Garden in Myth, Religion and Art
Glorification: Religious Abstraction in Renaissance and 20th Century Art
Early Netherlandish Painting
Leonardo da Vinci
Piero della Francesca
Giovanni Bellini
Fra Angelico: Art and Religion in the Renaissance
Mark Rothko: The Art of Transcendence

Frank Stella: American Abstract Artist
Jasper Johns
Brice Marden
Alison Wilding: The Embrace of Sculpture
Vincent van Gogh: Visionary Landscapes
Eric Gill: Nuptials of God

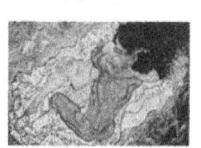

Constantin Brancusi: Sculpting the Essence of Things
Max Beckmann
Caravaggio
Gustave Moreau
Egon Schiele: Sex and Death In Purple Stockings
Delizioso Fotografico Fervore: Works In Process 1
Sacro Cuore: Works In Process 2
The Light Eternal: J.M.W. Turner
The Madonna Glorified: Karen Arthurs

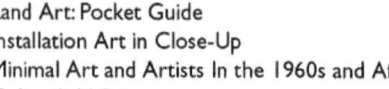

LITERATURE

J.R.R. Tolkien: The Books, The Films, The Whole Cultural Phenomenon
J.R.R. Tolkien: Pocket Guide
Tolkien's Heroic Quest
The *Earthsea* Books of Ursula Le Guin
Beauties, Beasts and Enchantment: Classic French Fairy Tales
German Popular Stories by the Brothers Grimm
Philip Pullman and *His Dark Materials*
Sexing Hardy: Thomas Hardy and Feminism
Thomas Hardy's *Tess of the d'Urbervilles*
Thomas Hardy's *Jude the Obscure*
Thomas Hardy: The Tragic Novels
Love and Tragedy: Thomas Hardy
The Poetry of Landscape in Hardy
Wessex Revisited: Thomas Hardy and John Cowper Powys
Wolfgang Iser: Essays and Interviews
Petrarch, Dante and the Troubadours
Maurice Sendak and the Art of Children's Book Illustration
Andrea Dworkin
Cixous, Irigaray, Kristeva: The *Jouissance* of French Feminism
Julia Kristeva: Art, Love, Melancholy, Philosophy, Semiotics and Psychoanalysis
Hélène Cixous I Love You: The *Jouissance* of Writing
Luce Irigaray: Lips, Kissing, and the Politics of Sexual Difference
Peter Redgrove: Here Comes the Flood
Peter Redgrove: Sex-Magic-Poetry-Cornwall
Lawrence Durrell: Between Love and Death, East and West
Love, Culture & Poetry: Lawrence Durrell
Cavafy: Anatomy of a Soul
German Romantic Poetry: Goethe, Novalis, Heine, Hölderlin
Feminism and Shakespeare
Shakespeare: Love, Poetry & Magic
The Passion of D.H. Lawrence
D.H. Lawrence: Symbolic Landscapes
D.H. Lawrence: Infinite Sensual Violence
Rimbaud: Arthur Rimbaud and the Magic of Poetry
The Ecstasies of John Cowper Powys
Sensualism and Mythology: The Wessex Novels of John Cowper Powys
Amorous Life: John Cowper Powys and the Manifestation of Affectivity (H.W. Fawkner)
Postmodern Powys: New Essays on John Cowper Powys (Joe Boulter)
Rethinking Powys: Critical Essays on John Cowper Powys
Paul Bowles & Bernardo Bertolucci
Rainer Maria Rilke
Joseph Conrad: *Heart of Darkness*
In the Dim Void: Samuel Beckett
Samuel Beckett Goes into the Silence
André Gide: Fiction and Fervour
Jackie Collins and the Blockbuster Novel
Blinded By Her Light: The Love-Poetry of Robert Graves
The Passion of Colours: Travels In Mediterranean Lands
Poetic Forms

POETRY

Ursula Le Guin: Walking In Cornwall
Peter Redgrove: Here Comes The Flood
Peter Redgrove: Sex-Magic-Poetry-Cornwall
Dante: Selections From the Vita Nuova
Petrarch, Dante and the Troubadours
William Shakespeare: Sonnets
William Shakespeare: Complete Poems
Blinded By Her Light: The Love-Poetry of Robert Graves
Emily Dickinson: Selected Poems
Emily Brontë: Poems
Thomas Hardy: Selected Poems
Percy Bysshe Shelley: Poems
John Keats: Selected Poems
Joh n Keats: Poems of 1820
D.H. Lawrence: Selected Poems
Edmund Spenser: Poems
Edmund Spenser: Amoretti
John Donne: Poems
Henry Vaughan: Poems
Sir Thomas Wyatt: Poems
Robert Herrick: Selected Poems
Rilke: Space, Essence and Angels in the Poetry of Rainer Maria Rilke
Rainer Maria Rilke: Selected Poems
Friedrich Hölderlin: Selected Poems
Arseny Tarkovsky: Selected Poems
Arthur Rimbaud: Selected Poems
Arthur Rimbaud: A Season in Hell
Arthur Rimbaud and the Magic of Poetry
Novalis: Hymns To the Night
German Romantic Poetry
Paul Verlaine: Selected Poems
Elizaethan Sonnet Cycles
D.J. Enright: By-Blows
Jeremy Reed: Brigitte's Blue Heart
Jeremy Reed: Claudia Schiffer's Red Shoes
Gorgeous Little Orpheus
Radiance: New Poems
Crescent Moon Book of Nature Poetry
Crescent Moon Book of Love Poetry
Crescent Moon Book of Mystical Poetry
Crescent Moon Book of Elizabethan Love Poetry
Crescent Moon Book of Metaphysical Poetry
Crescent Moon Book of Romantic Poetry
Pagan America: New American Poetry

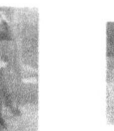

MEDIA, CINEMA, FEMINISM and CULTURAL STUDIES

J.R.R. Tolkien: The Books, The Films, The Whole Cultural Phenomenon
J.R.R. Tolkien: Pocket Guide
The *Lord of the Rings* Movies: Pocket Guide
The Cinema of Hayao Miyazaki
Hayao Miyazaki: *Princess Mononoke*: Pocket Movie Guide
Hayao Miyazaki: *Spirited Away*: Pocket Movie Guide
Tim Burton : Hallowe'en For Hollywood
Ken Russell
Ken Russell: *Tommy*: Pocket Movie Guide
The Ghost Dance: The Origins of Religion
The Peyote Cult
Cixous, Irigaray, Kristeva: The *Jouissance* of French Feminism
Julia Kristeva: Art, Love, Melancholy, Philosophy, Semiotics and Psychoanalysis
Luce Irigaray: Lips, Kissing, and the Politics of Sexual Difference
Hélène Cixous I Love You: The *Jouissance* of Writing
Andrea Dworkin
'Cosmo Woman': The World of Women's Magazines
Women in Pop Music
HomeGround: The Kate Bush Anthology
Discovering the Goddess (Geoffrey Ashe)
The Poetry of Cinema
The Sacred Cinema of Andrei Tarkovsky
Andrei Tarkovsky: Pocket Guide
Andrei Tarkovsky: *Mirror*: Pocket Movie Guide
Andrei Tarkovsky: *The Sacrifice*: Pocket Movie Guide
Walerian Borowczyk: Cinema of Erotic Dreams
Jean-Luc Godard: The Passion of Cinema
Jean-Luc Godard: *Hail Mary*: Pocket Movie Guide
Jean-Luc Godard: *Contempt*: Pocket Movie Guide
Jean-Luc Godard: *Pierrot le Fou*: Pocket Movie Guide
John Hughes and Eighties Cinema
Ferris Bueller's Day Off: Pocket Movie Guide
Jean-Luc Godard: Pocket Guide
The Cinema of Richard Linklater
Liv Tyler: Star In Ascendance
Blade Runner and the Films of Philip K. Dick
Paul Bowles and Bernardo Bertolucci
Media Hell: Radio, TV and the Press
An Open Letter to the BBC
Detonation Britain: Nuclear War in the UK
Feminism and Shakespeare
Wild Zones: Pornography, Art and Feminism
Sex in Art: Pornography and Pleasure in Painting and Sculpture
Sexing Hardy: Thomas Hardy and Feminism

CRESCENT MOON PUBLISHING
P.O. Box 1312, Maidstone, Kent, ME14 5XU, Great Britain. www.crmoon.com

cresmopub@yahoo.co.uk   www.crescentmoon.org.uk